Fear Dreams

A Novel

J.A. Schneider

For Bob, Matt, Danielle, Jean and Louise

Fear Dreams

1.

The water was green. Swirling and thick with stirred-up silt. Too hard to see through, so her eyes squeezed shut but not fast enough. The blue shirt was drifting closer. It shouldn't have been there in the water, Paul said they'd go away, these things she kept seeing, but the current smacked the shirt tight to her face and she couldn't breathe. Her chest heaved, struggling for air, and then she woke, shaking, covered with sweat.

The heart, oh the heart, it hammered. Liddy gulped a ragged breath as she rolled to a dryer place on the pillow. Her eyes blinked, still seeing that shirt sweep away. Gone. Lost to someone.

For long moments she lay, waiting for the banging in her chest to slow. Then…

On the bed table sat a note. Liddy groaned and reached for it; read; put it back. Two crutches leaned on the near chair.

"Done with you," she whispered to them. She'd been run over on June third. Her clock next to the note said it was August tenth. Nine weeks since the accident.

Be happy you're alive, she kept hearing. Right, *be thankful*, she stormed at herself, fighting tears because of the damned dream. The cast was off, wasn't it? The doctor said walk, gentle exercise. Rehab said ditto. Ten days ago she'd graduated from the track thing with the rails, walked all the way to the cake Reenie and Carol got for her to celebrate. Started to cry when they hugged her.

She was tired of crying, just sick of it. Today would be good if she had to break her leg all over again – whoops, crazy thought, watch that, don't slide again. But isn't it amazing, how relative things are? She was going out today, woo hoo, getting out of this drab place and apartment-hunting no less, and if she had to climb stairs or stumble off some curb it was her choice as opposed to having some drunk run her down. She stared at nothing; saw those terrifying headlights come at her again with their frantic horn blaring - but she shut it down fast; with something like a childish whimper forced her mind back to today.

She'd been learning to do that. Shut down bad things. But that wasn't helping her memory come back, was it? Alex her shrink said that was counterproductive, she had to face the bad stuff in order to - oh screw Alex. She wanted to be happy. Today would be good. It had to be.

With a groan she got herself up, hobbled – mornings were the worst – to move the crutches to the back of the closet, then went into the bathroom. In the shower, the hot water stung her face and stiff body. Felt nice. Steam rose and billowed. Droplets started to cry down the glass wall.

Liddy stared.

Stopped shampooing. Her soapy fingers went to the glass, touched the face. A weeping face that melted under more droplets, then disappeared.

Push it *down*, just imagination, Liddy thought minutes later, holding her hair dryer. That's what comes from spending too much time alone, in the apartment, in your head. Her mother used to tell her she had an overactive imagination. Paul still said that, but he understood. She was an artist, everything was visual; subconscious visual often saw and felt what surface minds didn't. Paul the logical, facts-bound scientist was fascinated by creative people. "A painting?" he'd say. "You see what *isn't there yet* and make it."

Liddy reached to wipe the mirror; saw dark circles under dark eyes that hadn't been sleeping enough. I used to be pretty, she thought, sighing – and then the hair dryer stopped. Just like that, switched off. She frowned at it, fiddled with its buttons. Nothing. She reached up to the plug, adjusted it – "Oh!" – and sparks zapped and flashed. Frightened, she drew back; put the dryer down. Left her hair half wet and hobbled back to the bedroom.

Someone was arguing somewhere. She went to pull aside the curtains and peered out. A woman's angry voice and then a man's, going at it from one of those windows across the way. Which one?

Liddy leaned to see, her heart thudding again. Nutty reaction but she couldn't help it. Some couple probably just having a tiff…

She felt his arm reach past her cheek and hug across her chest. He loved to sneak up. "How's my girl?"

"Argh, you scared me!"

She turned to Paul, inhaled and melted into him. They kissed; then she buried her face in his shoulder, remembering their love-making last night. Gentle and sweet, he'd been so careful not to hurt her. Out of habit, she reached to pat down a cowlick in his dark hair that was usually messy. He needed a haircut.

"Some couple over there is fighting," she said.

"Who?" Paul leaned and his large hazel eyes looked past her. Across the way, on West 83rd with a narrow space between for a lower building, the windows were all blank with shades pulled halfway, air conditioner boxes rattling on this hot and sleepy August Sunday.

"I don't see nuttin," he teased, straightening. "You sure you heard with those ACs going?" His smile was wonderful as he held up his bakery bag. "Find my note?"

"Yes, mmm, smells wonderful." Liddy smiled.

"Fresh croissants and bagels." He put his arm around her. "You good? Feets moving? C'mon, let's eat."

2.

In the kitchen he sat her down, piled the bakery eats into a linen-napkin-lined basket, and reached for the coffee. "Dig in," he said, pouring into her cup. "You sure you're up for today?"

"Oh yeah," she replied. "I am so ready to get out."

"Cool," he said, sounding a little ridiculous since before all *this* it was hardly a typical response. He was a serious scientist, bordering on nerdy if he weren't good-looking, but since the accident he'd been practically straining to be "up" and encouraging. He'd hauled back her easel, draftsman's table, and art supplies from the studio she'd been co-renting with other artists in an old warehouse on West 47th. Tons of effort, and it hadn't helped her much emotionally. One day, having no luck with her painting and hurting in her pillow-piled chair, Liddy cried to move out of their stodgy Upper West Side to a more artistic neighborhood. Soho? Tribeca? She'd asked before in the over four years they'd been married and he'd balked - those neighborhoods were more expensive – but on the day she cried he'd practically flown out the door. Made forays and looked at apartments and warmed to the idea. Paul Barron, neuroscientist, was suddenly not that guy in the white coat obsessing about Halothane and Propofol and molecular weights and formulas. He'd been talking to Soho-ites; announced that he liked the vibe and was discovering his artistic side, too. Lo, now he was smearing butter across his croissant and calling it a comet.

"Beth called while you were asleep," he said, turning on their kitchen TV, flipping around, muttering "news, same old news."

"What's the word?" Liddy nibbled a raisin bagel.

"Three new elevator places in Soho she wants to show us. You didn't like any of the others she showed me?"

"Liked them, didn't love them." The places he'd seen with Beth Liddy had seen online. Studied every room, little terrace, nook and cranny.

"Okay, well these sound good." Paul turned off the TV, pulled a map of lower Manhattan closer. "Two just reduced their prices, last minute hoping to grab people trying to get settled before school begins. August is a good time to move."

"Elevators make places more expensive and I told Beth I don't need one."

"Your leg."

"I'm *healed*. Just stiff in the mornings and at my drawing board sometimes. Besides, they've got me doing stairs at rehab."

Bethany Harms was Liddy's friend from their art school days who'd decided she was a no-talent, had given up becoming the next Georgia O'Keefe for the artistic thrill of selling real estate. Paul was reading some notes he'd scribbled from her call. "One place on Mercer – kinda expensive…a loft on Greene Street, price not terrible, third place on Sullivan - oh, she did mention a loft on Prince Street that's less expensive but unfortunately a walkup. Third floor."

"Let's take the walkup." Liddy said; then hesitated, meeting Paul's eyes as if suddenly feeling guilty. She hated the fact that she was timid. Why couldn't she be like other women and say, Dammit, I want to move!

"I still feel bad," she said. "I pressured you into this."

"Nahhh." Paul smiled and got up for more coffee.

They'd discussed it before, and Paul was adamant. They'd saved from the years that they'd stayed here in what had been his bachelor pad, and he and his workaholic research partner Carl Finn were close to a breakthrough at the lab with Big Pharma salivating. Their work was at NYU anyway, just blocks north of Soho – why hadn't *he* thought of this?

"And big news," Paul said with a flair as he re-filled each of their mugs, made a fuss stirring in just the amount of milk Liddy liked. "I'm going to sell the boat."

Liddy stared at him. "You're kidding."

"Nope. It'll sell fast and it's equity till it does. It was a ridiculous expense anyway."

"But you love that boat." It was a thirty-four foot sailboat named Seafarer that had belonged to Paul's father, and was all he had. A sad man, he'd practically lived in it after his divorce, had spent his winters sailing to Key West where he'd lived like a bum, then had sailed up and down the Florida coast before drinking himself to death.

Liddy looked fretfully out their kitchen window. It offered a glimpse of the Hudson if you leaned out. "Now I feel doubly bad. You're selling the boat for me, aren't you? So we can afford Soho."

"No. It's just time to move on, evolve." He squeezed her hand, then went back to his map of lower Manhattan.

"It's why you moved here in the first place, to be close to it," Liddy fretted. They were just five blocks from the 79th Street boat basin.

Paul waved a hand.

"We've enjoyed the boat but we need a bigger place anyway, and why shouldn't it be where you'll be happier and I'll be closer to work? The restaurants in Soho, my God. This could be a blast."

"Carl would have to find another boat to borrow," Liddy said drily.

"Yeah well..." Paul shrugged and checked his watch. "Beth wants to meet us in forty minutes. Think we can make it?"

3.

Thirty blocks away, just before noon, all hell broke loose at the West 54th Street police station. Two detectives were already turning the air blue as others showed up for the bad news, and Kerri Blasco paced with her face crumpling. "How could this happen? *How the hell could this happen?*"

Her partner Alex Brand touched her arm as she flew past, half weeping as she turned, paced back, and stopped before their squad room's monitor. The others gave her looks that were just as frustrated as they resumed watching the tape, the whole catastrophic arrest scene that had wrecked months of work. The vile, sadistic psycho who raped and brutally beat his victims to death was going to walk free - on a technicality! Witness statements down the drain. Weeks of canvassing, police affidavits and warrants and stakeouts without number, a whole case Kerri and Alex had built, down the drain.

Buck Dillon, another homicide detective, gave Kerri a sympathetic tilt of his head that said hey, they're hurting too.

She exhaled hard. Yeah, they were hurting. Slumped in their chairs, two uniformed young cops who had chased and caught the slime, subdued him sustaining injuries as they grappled him face down onto the hood of their patrol car - best place, right in front of their dash cam. The tape was running, the audio blared yells and obscenities as one of them hollered the Miranda.

"You have the right to remain silent…"

Groaning obscenities about their mothers as the sicko's scraped, bleeding head bounced around.

"Anything you say…if you cannot afford an attorney…*do you understand?*"

More yelling, and the filthy, sweaty head of Ray Gruner bobbed as it dropped to the hood.

They'd brought him in. Given him soda and wiped the scrape on his lolling head. He hadn't requested a lawyer, and since he hated women Kerri had gone in alone to interrogate him. The tape had just reached that part. Kerri's heart pounded. She'd been exhausted and sleepless before this, so decided to drop into a chair too; for a whole minute watched herself with Gruner in the interview room. Couldn't stand it. Got up again and resumed pacing. Watching, hearing herself.

"You like to hurt women?"

Gruner leaned back, his pale, inhuman eye-slits mocking her. He was cuffed but managed to bulge his steroid pumped muscles under his black T-shirt.

"I *asked*, do you like to hurt women?"

His lips curled into a sneer. Bad teeth. He reeked in the small room.

"Makes you feel powerful, huh? Making women bleed, beating them to death?"

He thought that was funny. Rolled his eyes as if recalling fun times. "Blow me," he spat.

Kerri laid her folder on the table. Opened it, withdrew a paper document and a photo, slid the paper across the table to him.

"Your mother did tricks too, didn't she?" Kerri tapped the paper.

The smirk disappeared. Became an icy, killer glare.

"You lived with her in a one-bedroom. You were five when she was first arrested. Where'd she leave you when she was balling her clients? On the couch, maybe? On the other side of the thin wall where you could hear everything?"

He shifted. The corners of his mouth turned down, way down. His phosphorescent eye-slits glared at Kerri's throat, then south to her open-collared white blouse. She'd pulled her dark blond hair out of her ponytail and let it drop past her shoulders. She was about the same age – thirty-four – his mother had been when she was robbed and shot by one of her johns. Now Kerri pushed his mother's photo to him.

"She was pretty, wasn't she?" Kerri leaned further across the table, closer to him. "Big, smiling, beguiling eyes. Did you wish she paid more attention to you? Did you *hear* the moans and bouncing and thudding of the sex she was giving?"

He glared.

"As you got older, did you wish you were in bed there with her? Did you wish you, too, *were in her*, like all those men who came and didn't give a shit for you?"

His chair crashed back as he lunged, shrieking, "Bitch! I'd kill you *worse* than I did that Selena whore. I'd twist your arms off first!"

The others were on him fast, forcing him back down. They had him. Kerri remembered gulping her breath back in giant heaves and leaving the room thrilled. Another evil was removed from the streets. Now they could rejoice, catch up on sleep, grin to each other on hard teamwork finally ending well.

Until their Lieutenant Tom Mackey, with a sorry, frustrated face, saw the tape and shook his head.

Gruner hadn't been properly Mirandized. The unis who'd taken him down had pounded him. Yes, yes, his head bobbed and dropped during the Miranda, but *was that a nod?* For sure it wasn't a verbal yes. It could be argued that they'd beaten him into a confession.

They were screwed. It was over. Someone muttered that a public defender had arrived and was taking Gruner out, back to the streets. Someone else switched off the monitor. Silence closed in on the whole squad room, beyond depressing.

Depression becomes a wave that rises up and swallows you. Drags you down. Tells you that all your best and most desperate efforts are worthless. They all felt it, but Kerri Blasco had an easier time letting tears come.

4.

She made it to her desk, her piled-high, littered desk, and fell back in her chair. Through a stinging blur she scowled at stacked files, ME reports, witness statements from other open cases. *So many.* Face it: the system favors bad guys, lets them slip through the cracks more than half the bleeping time. She wanted to let out a good, self-indulgent, wonderfully howling bawl, but instead reached and whacked over her red papier-mâché pen holder. Ballpoints spilled to the floor.

"Oh, that's really going to help."

Alex Brand had been on his way back to his desk facing her, and knelt to pick up the scattered ballpoints. "Pencils too?" he said, rising, shoving his fist full of Bics and stubby pencils back into their holder. "Who still uses pencils?"

"People who wanna chew 'em," Kerri groused. "Don't interrupt my tantrum."

Ah, sweet Alex. Tough and terrific cop, feeling lousy like the rest of them but kneeling again now near her black Nikes for a last ballpoint he had missed. Once, they loved each other - a bad idea on top of Department Don'ts since Alex was married at the time and Kerri was struggling through a divorce. Since then they'd managed to contain their feelings, pretty much. They'd each gone through pain and needed peace for a while. Plus they'd been partners for nearly two years, which can lead anyone to sometimes bickering like old marrieds.

Do I still love him? Kerri often asked herself.

Of course I do. It always came back to her like that, a slam to the heart.

But how did he feel? Had he moved past that dangerous, red-hot attraction of twenty months ago?

If so, he had it too well under control, had recognized his aversion to drama. But he still cared about her, no doubt about that. He worried out loud, got sometimes downright fretful. "Hey, I'm a cop, remember?" she'd remind him, and he'd mutter, "Yeah, yeah," and wave a hand. Anyway, he was seeing someone else, although he hadn't mentioned her lately. Kerri wondered how that was going…

…and leaned down to him, to his flopping brown hair that needed a cut and had started to curl at his collar. He smiled at her, his hazel eyes urging her to feel better.

"You're a good man, Charlie Brown," she told him.

He got to his feet. "Nah. Mark Twain said the best way to cheer yourself is to cheer someone else, so I'm being selfish." He cracked another smile, went to his own desk and sat facing her. Poked at his files for a few seconds, then raised his eyes back to her. She looked really tired. Still pretty, now pulling her hair back into its usual ponytail, but there were dark circles under her dark blue eyes and her tall, slender frame looked suddenly thinner. The collar of her white blouse looked too big on her; ditto the pants of her black pants suit.

"Take a day, Kerri. Go home. What little sleep you've gotten has been up in the crib. Don't you have plants to water or something?"

As Sergeant he was also her boss, telling her nicely before pressing harder as he sometimes had to do. Kerri knew the boundaries of their give and take; knew too when she could say no.

"Home is lonely. The plants are watered and the cat has enough Meow Mix for a week." She pulled some folders to her and opened the top two. "I'll just do some of this cheery light reading to decompress," she said, letting out a pent-up sigh. "That hedge funder who says he didn't drown his wife in the bathtub. That mother of the year who says her kid fell accidentally off the fire escape."

Abruptly, she got up. "But first I shower. Yech, that reeking, murdering POS touched me."

He caught her arm as she started past. "We'll still get him. They're going to be sitting on him every move he makes. He'll make another mistake and we'll get him."

"Will he have to murder someone else first?" she grimaced. It obsessed her that women were so easy to harm.

Jo Babiak, another detective, came and put a new folder on Kerri's desk. "Unpleasant update on that missing coed," she said. "They're about to close the case, declare her a runaway."

Kerri frowned at the folder's label: Sasha Perry. "No way. That's a homicide."

Jo shrugged unhappily. "Agreed, but hard to prove with no body. She disappeared in June."

Kerri flipped open the folder. A blonde looked up at her from what would have been her graduation photo: pretty, delicate-looking with a crooked smile. Anger re-took the hurting detective's heart, which was good, it was a fast cure for depression. "There is no way this girl wanted to die or disappear," Kerri said bitterly. "She was thrilled about graduating. Wanted to become a vet - *rescued animals*, for God's sake."

"Yeah, this one hurts," Jo said, catching Alex's grim head shake that said he felt the same. Over two months, Sasha Perry had been missing. Everything pointed to foul play but there was no way to prove it; it was hard, even, to investigate. The P.D. had really worked this, tried to build a case, collected hundreds of witness statements but were left with big holes.

Sasha had been a student at NYU. It was August. Friends and friends of friends were scattered. Funds had run out for this. The door was about to close and every detective in the squad now worried about Kerri, who'd become obsessed with the case. Was found, after double shifts, exhausted and still poring over evidence, rereading witness statements, getting nowhere.

They had taken turns helping her when they could, but they'd all started to shake their heads. Gotta give it up, Kerri...

Gently, she straightened Sasha Perry's photo in the folder, then closed it and placed it on her desk. "I'm going to shower and be back in five minutes," she said. "Can we talk more about this?"

Alex was now on his phone, but Jo said yes. "In an hour if I don't get called. That woman who says she didn't kill her boyfriend-"

Her phone went off too. She answered, rolled her eyes at Kerri. She and her partner Buck Dillon had been called out.

Kerri rushed off, in a hurry to be back.

5.

Beth Harms, surprisingly, tried to veto the Prince Street loft, on the grounds that it was "trouble."

As undergraduates, Beth had served as the pragmatic brakes to Liddy's too-easy leaps from practicality. They'd become friends in one of their art history classes; had bonded further in their studio art and over boyfriend and financial troubles and Beth's divorce and years of struggling to get gallery representation. Beth was a born New Yorker, with her healthy cynicism built in. Liddy came from a small town upstate, the youngest in a family often too busy or overwhelmed to pay much attention to her, so she'd grown up lonely, in her own world, reading and sketching compulsively. Even now, as they met first at a sidewalk cafe on Soho's Spring Street, Liddy's hand zoomed her charcoal pencil around in one of the sketchbooks she carried everywhere.

Paul wanted to know why the loft would be trouble. "The price sounds right."

"Well…" Beth put down her lemonade, still admiring Liddy's sketch of a dark-haired woman who had passed them minutes before. "Amazing," she said. "You only caught a glimpse of her."

"But she was so striking." Liddy smudged charcoal into the lines of the woman's dark eyes. Her hand worked. Beth turned back to Paul.

"For starters, the place is going to need work. The owner trashed it. Charlie Bass, ever hear of him?"

They hadn't.

"He was a troubled actor who had a role in that whatchamacallit vampire movie, and he…ah, hung himself. The joist is still there, *bent* where he did it."

14

Liddy's hand holding her pencil stopped motionless. "How awful."

"But it's near," Paul said, finding a voicemail on his phone, cursing that it was Carl Finn his research partner probably wondering where he was. "If we don't see the place we'll be curious."

He rose and paced near the shade of their umbrella to argue into his phone about "different mechanisms" and "modify the compound" and "Propofol analogue, it's the analogue!"

Beth watched him for a moment. "Carl's working today?" she asked Liddy. "It's *Sunday*."

"He's manic."

"Back on uppers?"

"Up, down, up, down."

"He's an M.D. Nice when you can prescribe for yourself."

"Definitely. So…the loft?"

Beth leaned closer. "It isn't *that* bad," she said low. "Just depressing even for me, and I'm the listing broker and – given those awful dreams you've been having…"

"They're lessening."

"Lessening but more intense when they happen. You told me."

"Yes but…" Liddy inhaled, seeing her fear dream of this morning flashing in her mind for just a second, then disappearing. The day was bright and sunny; it felt so euphoric to be out. "We could make the loft beautiful," she said, back to sketching. Now working on another woman's face, this one younger, maybe twenty, a delicate-looking blonde with a crooked smile.

"Who's that?"

"She just walked by too."

"Uh, *her* I would have noticed. She's a magazine cover."

"You were watching Paul. I saw her for a split second."

Beth peered at Liddy a bit open-mouthed; incongruously looked up and down the busy sidewalk and across the narrow street with its colorful jaywalkers. She hadn't seen the blonde. "Well, that sketch is even more gorgeous. Hey, the charcoal's going to smudge. You gonna spray it?"

Liddy did. Got out her Krylon fixative for pastel and chalk and sprayed both drawings, flipping from the older, dark-haired woman to the girl with the crooked smile.

Then stared at her, touched her cheek and then her delicate brow; seemed suddenly forlorn. Beth frowned and reached for her scrapbook, angled it on the table so she could study the girl's face.

"I've seen her before."

"Right. She just walked past."

"I mean before today. Like, on TV or something."

"Maybe she's a model." Liddy's eyes stayed on the girl; now seemed almost lost as she angled her sketchbook back. Her expression bothered Beth. It was how she'd looked in the days and weeks after her accident.

"Lids? When was your last nightmare? And *headache?* Hey, you had a concussion, too."

No answer. A car had honked and someone called out to it, but Beth was sure Liddy heard. She leaned closer.

"Fess up. *Tell.*"

Liddy snapped out of it. The question was painful, so she looked out to the sunny street with its colorful commotion and a daisy-decorated bakery van and a man carrying brightly painted mannequins. "The headaches are fewer," she finally said. "And this morning was another dream but they're getting further and further apart too and I'm feeling better, really."

"Okay, what about your memory?"

"Things are coming back."

"Paul said so, he's thrilled."

"Yesterday for the third time I went out for groceries. Got off at the *right* floor, imagine that. Not the wrong floor, wandering

16

around wondering why I couldn't find our door. I also remember where my sock drawer is and no longer replace the milk next to the Cheerios or the soup cans. I'd love to see that loft."

6.

It was one of those narrow old cast-iron buildings Soho is famous for, painted the color of red brick with huge, arching windows. On the stairs, which Liddy took slowly, they passed workmen coming down carrying Sheetrock panels and electrical wiring. Construction, Beth explained, was underway on the fourth floor, and she snickered. "Construction's *always* going on around here. Everyone has to have their own unique vision, blah, blah. Oh, and the first and second floors are owned by some rich guy from Shanghai who's seldom here. You'd have the building practically to yourselves."

Paul climbing up behind Liddy said, "Until the fourth floor people move in."

"Which will be a while," Beth answered. "You should *see* what they're doing up there."

At the end of a short hall on the third floor landing, she turned the key in the door, pushed it open, and punched off the security system. "After you, please," she announced, hoity toity as if showing around her usual artsy types. "Watch your step."

It was a bright but dusty artist's loft, still partially furnished, the floor gritty with piles of ground gypsum plaster where poor Charlie Bass had apparently taken a sledge hammer to what was left of an interior wall. Otherwise the space was mostly open with exposed wooden beams, original cast iron columns painted white, and three huge arched windows facing south. Beth turned up the air conditioning, then droned almost reluctantly about the "two bedrooms, two baths, great kitchen," but Liddy rushed – the fastest she'd moved in weeks - to the arched window furthest on the right.

"Ohh," she burst out, shielding her eyes from the brilliant sun and looking around. Below, bustling Prince Street. To her right and brushing her shoulder, huge plants - ficus trees, a rubber plant, smaller hanging ferns, and what looked like a lemon tree – and to her left, a telescope. Paul, coming up behind her, fingered the telescope, bent to examine the tripod it was mounted on, then rose to the telescope again.

"Hey, a Celestron Omni," he said. "Nice. You could see Mars with this." He peered into it; moved the 'scope barrel up, then down.

Beth said, "Charlie Bass was a peeping tom. Considered the windows across the street better entertainment than cable."

Paul thought that was funny and kept peering through the telescope. Liddy asked, "Who's been watering the plants?"

"I have. See that little hose running into the wall? And this spray bottle?" She bent to it. "Despite the air conditioning the leaves fry this close to the glass and need spraying." Hurriedly, she sprayed some of the leaves, put the bottle back behind the rubber plant's tub, and straightened. "Charlie called this his greenhouse and apparently loved it. Told pals his dream was to run a real greenhouse someday, get out of trying to make it in the nasty, crazy film world."

She sighed, turned and looked back to the furniture still in the room. "His executor says a lot of his stuff is for sale."

"The telescope?" Paul asked.

"The plants?" from Liddy.

"Yes and yes." Beth looked toward a doorway. "Want to see the rest of the place?"

They walked past the white columns and an exposed brick wall to the kitchen, never-used-looking all white with granite counter tops and laundry/dryer and an all-purpose center island. The master bedroom was large, nearly its whole wall another arched window now half covered with drooping, smeared drapes.

19

At the sight of the second, smaller bedroom Liddy cried "Oh, Paul," found his hand and squeezed it. He said "Mm" noncommittally, but squeezed back.

It faced north, would be a perfect studio with shelves already built in, a three-sided window seat nestled into more floor-to-ceiling shelves, and a long, east-west wall perfect for drying canvases.

Beth muttered, "I was afraid you'd like it."

Liddy spread her arms, as if to take in and embrace the whole loft. "I *love* it, it's marvelous! We can fix it and make it beautiful and replace poor Charlie Bass's darkness with light!"

"Speaking of Charlie," Paul said. "Where did he, uh…"

Beth showed them.

In the living area not far from the plants, she pointed to a ceiling joist running under one of the wooden beams. "There," she said.

The joist was tubular metal, still bent raggedly. Tragic to look at. A terrible downer reminding them of a sad, troubled life that ended badly.

Liddy stared at the joist. Her heart started pounding, and the oddest feeling came to her that Charlie was there in the room, reaching out to her. Where had that come from? She didn't know. She felt sorrow and…something else; looked around, then looked at the others as if trying to explain her feelings to herself.

"I feel connected to this place. That studio? Charlie made it like a cozy cave for a hermit who loved to read. And his plants…I love plants." She looked back to the foliage. "You missed some ferns, Beth, they *are* frying."

She went for the plastic bottle and started to spray ferns and other leafy branches. Paul came next to her, fingering the telescope as she sprayed, up, down, back up, inadvertently hitting the window's glass as droplets slid and coalesced and then…lit up in colors.

"A rainbow!" Liddy exclaimed. "Ohh…" The glowing arc shimmered, then changed into something like back-lit stained glass, then melted as droplets dripped down, and were gone. The glass still steamed and glowed.

"Pretty," Beth said.

Softly, Liddy said, "This place speaks to me."

Paul said dubiously, "Today this place is cheery with the sun pouring in. But picture it when it's dark and gloomy, and your painting isn't going well or you've had one of your clients reject your hard work or you've had *another one of your dreams*. What then?"

It didn't penetrate, his words seemed like white noise. Liddy kept staring out, then down to the street again. She felt mesmerized, thrilled. "It's cheaper than those places you've already looked at," she said, trying to sound as if practical considerations stood foremost in her mind. A force took greater hold and she found herself turning, looking back in the direction of the second bedroom.

"I could be happy in just that studio! Lock me up in it and it could be my happy little cell."

Beth made comic tugging motions on her sleeve. "Sleep on it, Lids. Come on, I've got other places to show you and you shouldn't tire."

On the way down they passed another couple coming up with another realtor Beth greeted. Liddy stopped at the landing below; looked fretfully up as the couple entered the loft.

"They're gonna take it," she whimpered the rest of the way down and on the sidewalk. And three apartments later – three elevator apartments later - exploring a place with a terrace on Sullivan, she looked anxiously out trying to see the Prince Street building. It frustrated her that she couldn't. She kept insisting, as they left the third place, how the Prince Street loft felt as if she already lived there and *had* been living there. It felt so perfect but that other couple was going to grab it! Or others would!

They almost argued as they stood thanking Beth on the corner of Moore Street.

"You said sleep on it," Liddy pleaded, "but it's too great a deal for that."

Beth repeated that the place's sad past and Liddy's fragile state and the fact that it was a walk-up were what worried her. Paul agreed, but also admitted to not being completely thrilled with any of the places he'd seen alone with Beth.

"You didn't like any of them?" Beth asked Liddy.

"Liked them, didn't love them," Liddy said.

"Maybe if you saw them for real instead of just online?"

Liddy shook her head, and Paul, grimacing, said, "I'm just afraid of jumping in too fast."

In the cab the pressure was palpable. Liddy looked tired, torn, and stared fretfully out. Paul hunched forward, fiddling with his cell phone.

The cab swerved, and he said suddenly, "You know what I want most?"

"What?" Liddy didn't turn.

"I want you to be happy and us to be settled, back ASAP to being able to concentrate on work. That was Carl who called while we were in the café."

"I heard."

"*He's* working today, and he worked late last night. Saturday night and he was the only one in the lab."

"He's obsessed."

"Obsessed gets the job done."

"So you'll both develop a breakthrough new anesthesia drug a week later."

"There's the time factor, Lids. We're under the gun."

"Oh right." Now she felt beaten. "So maybe we shouldn't move at all."

"Stop."

In his phone Paul studied a map of Soho, scrolling to the neighborhood of NYU just to the north. "Am I crazy for hesitating? You love the loft and Prince Street is just a few blocks from the lab. I can't even imagine being free of subways."

Heartened, Liddy grabbed his arm. "Oh, let's take it! It's a *wonderful* apartment! It was Hollywood that brought Charlie Bass down, destroyed him because he must have been too sensitive - but we can make it beautiful and *home*. Bring it back to life!"

Paul gave in to a grin and called Beth and told her they wanted the place. He turned his phone up to blast the reaction.

"Just in time, I checked that other couple and they were ready to bid! This is so great - after seeing Liddy's reaction I think she really will be happy there. Lemme talk to her! I'm thrilled!"

7.

The paperwork went fast, contracts were signed, and four days later Carl Finn came to see it. "Wow, you could flip this and make a fortune."

"We're not flipping it."

It was Thursday. Carl was tense about Paul's taking time off from the lab and he let it show. Liddy did her best to ignore him. She was using Paul's measurements of the living area to make sketches of where furniture would go. Over by the arched window, Paul was busy with Charlie Bass's executor, a solemn man in his sixties named Griffin who was pointing out things the estate wanted to sell and naming his prices, all of them low. Better than having herds of looky-loos charging in "to see where it happened," Griffin had said when they called him. He'd cared about Charlie, didn't want the disposal of his things turned into a circus. Charlie's suicide had been all over the media.

So Liddy had Carl standing over her while she sat, in her blouse and black jeans, scribbling designs on inexpensive paper. She had her regular sketchbook open next to her on the couch. Carl didn't sit. He paced and kept peering impatiently over to Paul.

"You're keeping this too?" he said, reaching to touch the couch's fabric inches from her. Once white and now soiled, the sofa would have to be re-covered but was still structurally beautiful: long and L-shaped with a matching ottoman, destined for wonderful coziness facing the television. Liddy nodded yes to Carl's question and kept scribbling. Keep moving, Carl. Go talk to Paul, Carl.

"Oh, these are nice." Now he bent to her scrapbook, flipping pages: a sketch she'd started of Mr. Griffin, the dark-haired woman of days ago, the young blonde, two children playing Liddy had sketched yesterday in Riverside Park.

"Who's that?" he asked, pointing to the young blonde.

"Just someone I saw."

"Where?"

"In the neighborhood."

"Pretty, looks familiar." Besides sailing when he got himself away from work, Carl's other hobby was women. They couldn't keep track of his girlfriends.

Peripherally, Liddy saw him straighten and look again to Paul and Mr. Griffin. "Going to buy that telescope too?"

"Yes, Paul likes it. Go check it out."

Carl moved away, tall and well built in his preppy chinos and blue polo shirt, running a hand through his dark hair as he bent to the 'scope and looked in. Spent maybe two minutes engrossed in the views of windows across the street until Paul turned and introduced him to Charlie's executor.

They were both from Connecticut and had been friends for years, Paul and Carl…which was only a bit unusual because Carl had been a rich kid from wealthy Greenwich, and Paul had been his boat boy. Scrubbed the hull, bartended his parties, cleaned his messes, even drove his drunk girlfriends home. Through family pull Carl got Paul a great scholarship, and Paul still felt indebted to him. Paul was now forty; Carl was forty-one, and had grown some surprise hang-ups in the intervening years. His father had lost his money in investments; Carl wasn't rich anymore and had lost his boat. Paul inherited *his* boat – his smaller boat - from his father, and they resumed their best buds bond of sailing. It was actually Carl who'd had the idea for the research they were doing, and snagged the grant – again, through family pull - and brought Paul in figuring two working feverishly could win the race to Big

Pharma. Carl was still mad at his banker cousins who'd scoffed when he opted for med school instead of finance. He was going to win bigger than them, oh yes – he was driven - and he'd done Paul another huge life favor with this research thing. He could have asked someone else.

"*I owe Carl everything.*" Liddy hated hearing Paul say that. He was brilliant too. He could have done okay on his own…

So forget them and their B.S., she thought, peering around, feeling her happy quotient rise, and then rise more. Wow, this was really happening.

She got herself up, aching only a little, appraising the emptiness and imagining the antique furniture they'd crowded into their old apartment moved to *there* and *there* - and those *gouges* in the wall - ugh, she thought, moving to one of them, reaching up to touch it. Construction people would be coming to fix it, also finish tearing down the interior wall poor Charlie Bass had taken a sledge hammer to. They'd restore the flooring and then painters would come and patch, spackle, prime and paint while Con Ed came too, and upholstery people to pick up the couch, ottoman and two other items…

"Lids?"

Uh-huh.

How well she knew Paul's regretful tone. She turned, knowing what was coming and went to them: to Paul looking sorry and Carl already eyeing the door and Mr. Griffin half turned away pushing papers back into his briefcase.

"Ah…" Paul started to say, and because she felt happy and he looked so guilty she waved a hand as if nothing.

"Let me guess," Liddy said. "Work's fallen behind and you really should leave now and may have to work late tonight."

"Well it *is* a week day," Carl said with a quick smile. He had quick eyes, too; quick and blue.

"I understand," she smiled, to Paul's clear relief. They had planned dinner out tonight, to celebrate their first day of owning the place and starting the refurbishing.

Paul spread his hands as if to say, What can I do? Carl smirked and dude-punched Paul's arm. "Right there," he said with his other hand pointing to Liddy, "is why I'm divorced and you're not. Cassie wouldn't tolerate my hours and that was that."

Cassie wouldn't tolerate…?

What a phony. Like a flash, Liddy remembered trying to help Paul with the rigging, and she was cold, it was gloomy and windy and she wanted to run below for her sweatshirt but Paul looked troubled. "They're down there." Carl and his current squeeze were down in the berth having their tryst, on Paul's boat, so she couldn't go for her damned sweatshirt. When was that? Last April? No…last fall maybe, there'd been other women since. He'd taken the boat out alone lots too. Said it helped re-charge his batteries.

There was a sudden movement toward the door, first saying good-bye and thank you to Mr. Griffin; then, with Carl already out in the hall, a quick hug from Paul with hurried promises to celebrate soon.

"*Every* night once we're done with this damned thing," he said, suddenly more emotional with Carl's footsteps pounding down the stairs. "The deadline for that presentation's in five weeks. It'll blow 'em away." He pushed a strand of hair from Liddy's brow. "Our copyright-sharing with the U will be assured and we'll be in clover. Sound good?"

"Heaven." She smiled and stood back from him, not unhappy at all at the thought of coming silence. "At least it's summer and neither of you have to teach."

That didn't cheer Paul. "Yeah, well y'know how fast September's going to be here? There's that pressure too; get as much done before we have to work teaching around it."

"Go. I'll be fine and busy here." Liddy held up her list of things to do.

"Cab home."

"Of course."

"Call me when you get there."

"Yes, yes." She hugged him again. "Soon *here* will be home, imagine! Everything's under control."

8.

She closed the door and breathed a sigh of relief. So much to do… She turned back to the room, and her feeling changed.

The place seemed suddenly cavernous, echoing with voices and footsteps no longer there. She tried to shake off the feeling. Went to get Paul's measuring tape from where he'd left it by the telescope. Knelt to measure the space between the couch and the wall where the flat screen would go – joy, the cozy place where they'd unwind and cuddle and forget the day's pressures…

On her knees, Liddy looked up. The compulsion she'd been resisting finally seized her. It was still there, the bent pipe where Charlie Bass had hung himself. Breath stopped as she stared at it, feeling a slow, cold dread overtake her. *Have them fix that first. Make it disappear…*

She rose and backed away, still staring at the pipe. Looked down and forced herself to turn. Get busy with something else, yes, that's the ticket. Now she faced the big arched window, ablaze with late sun shining through - and frying the leaves.

She hurried over and started to spray. Up, down, squirt, squirt, the ficus and the ferns, the lemon tree too. Her finger hurt from pulling the spray trigger; the bottle emptied fast. She knelt to the small hose and turned it on, started to refill the spray bottle.

Her phone rang, startling her. "Oh!"

Beth, sounding hyper. "I remember where I've seen that girl! The one you sketched in the café? She's that missing NYU coed."

Liddy was confused.

"I mean I *think* it's her, they just showed her photo on the news and it's been bugging me, like something it was important to remember."

Still kneeling, Liddy turned off the hose, put down the plastic bottle. Her sketchbook was a few feet away on a stool. She reached for it and opened it; found the page as Beth's voice continued.

"Blond and pretty, you said; walked past us only I didn't see her. I've been racking my brain thinking - wait, she's missing but suddenly she's seen just sauntering down a Soho street?" A pause; the sound of Beth's wheels turning almost audible.

"Then it occurred. Maybe you saw her picture *in the hospital*. You'd had a concussion and your leg was up in that sling thing but you were getting better, so maybe they turned on the TV - they were showing her in the news – and maybe *that's* where you saw her and remembered."

"What's her name?"

"Sasha Perry. Disappeared in early June."

"I'll google her. Wait a sec?"

"I'm here. Tearing around putting out crackers for an open house but I'll put you on speaker phone."

Liddy exited the call, went online on her phone and searched and there was Sasha Perry, her picture and thousands of hits. Her heart lurched in her chest; for long seconds she couldn't breathe.

She looked back up to the arched window. The leaves dripped. The sun glared hot through the glass.

Shakily she went back to her call. "You there?"

"Yup, I'm here." Beth's voice was yards away and then closer.

"*It was her.*" Liddy's voice caught as she immediately doubted herself. "I mean, I think it was, it looks like her." She rubbed her brow. "God, my mind is scrambled. So many things I don't remember right."

Beth's voice turned soft, encouraging. "But it's coming back, you said, right? Different memories are coming back?"

"Yeah." Liddy gave a mirthless laugh. "Stuff's filling in. I'm not mixing up my drawers anymore or leaving the fridge door open or forgetting how to tie my shoelaces. Alex said I'm getting better."

Alex Minton was the psychiatrist Liddy was seeing. *You're doing well for having gone through a traumatic experience,* he'd said on her last visit. *It's normal, totally human to struggle with forgetfulness, upsetting emotions, frightening dreams or a sense of danger. But you can speed your recovery with the right treatment, support and self-help strategy.*

She had pretty much memorized his words, which was odd: she seemed able to remember what she wanted to remember. Beth was babbling emotionally as Liddy peered around, thinking desperately that here – oh please, here - was going to be her self-help strategy.

"I could kick myself for getting you upset," Beth was saying. "I only called because the news said they're about to close the case and declare Sasha Perry a runaway, and if you *had* really seen her I was gonna say call the police? On the other hand it could have been someone who just *looked* like her."

"I don't know..."

Liddy's heart thudded as she looked up at the plants. The leaves dripped. Condensation on the glass formed a woman's face. Liddy gaped at it.

"You sound funny. You okay?"

The woman was young. Golden hair in the sun, woeful eyes that begged.

"You there? *Liddy?*"

"I'm here," she breathed, blinking. Stood to touch the face that wept, then melted into sliding tears. Liddy's heart rocketed. This is crazy, she told herself. Say nothing, you're just seeing things, Beth will fret you shouldn't have taken the loft. "I just feel bad, that's all," she finally managed. "It's so sad."

31

"You're sensitive. Sorry to sound like an amateur shrink, but that girl's face probably stuck in your subconscious because it's…another trauma and you identified. Maybe you saw her on this morning's news too?"

"Maybe. It was on but Paul turned it off."

"Well there you go. Hey, my mind plays tricks all the time."

"What would I do without you?"

"You're a survivor. Besides, you have Paul too."

"Yes. Paul too."

9.

They had ninety minutes. Just ninety bleeping minutes to grab a roach burger or even a halfway decent lunch but instead were doing *this*. Alex Brand sighed wearily, which made Kerri feel worse. The air conditioner in her six-year-old Bronco was only half working, they'd both been up most of the night with a drive-by shooting, and the traffic was barely moving under the broiling sun.

"This girl just got back from where?" Alex sighed again.

"Nigeria," Kerri said, driving, alternating between pressing a chilled Coke to her brow and wiping her sweating neck with an old T-shirt and cursing the whole month of August. "Her name's Becca Milstein. She's a first year med student, was a friend of Sasha Perry and just spent six weeks helping stop the spread of hepatitis B. Wound up getting sick. Wouldn't even be back already if she hadn't gotten sick."

"What kind of sick?"

"Fever of some sort."

"She say anything about ebola?"

"Didn't mention it."

"Did you *ask?*"

"Damn. Forgot."

They'd reached Greenwich Village. Alex glared out as Kerri swung east at Washington Square, heading past the lawn-surrounded, soaring water plumes of the Square's Fountain Plaza. When she hit Mercer and turned south again, he groaned for her to take him back to the fountain, whining *waaaater* like a movie cowboy crawling through the desert. He used cop humor a lot.

33

They all did; it helped some of the time. It also helped the feeling of uselessness to this trip downtown, since they were homicide cops and Sasha Perry had never been declared a homicide and the investigation done by others was hours from closing. Then that call had come from this med student. Despite sleep loss Kerri was newly excited. Volunteered her lunch hour. Had nearly run out alone when Alex who hated seeing her wreck her health over this volunteered to go with her.

He'd been more than supportive of her obsession with the case, but this was it - no more, Kerri, please? Others had done so much canvassing and interviewing and gathering witness statements. When he could and up till now, Alex had helped. Today was the first time he'd started to grumble.

"This med student – what's her name again?"

"Becca Milstein."

"Okay Becca. What are we doing, really? She didn't *say* anything concrete – just that she'd known Sasha and felt bad, felt she should call. That's sweet – but the oldest story is runaways who finally called home after months."

Kerri felt worse than she did five minutes ago. Alex was right; this would probably be just another wild goose chase, another hopeful lead that would peter out like a stuck balloon and leave her feeling about as effective as a busy fly in a jar. She sighed, pushed another Coke to him – they'd started with a six pack – and told him almost irritably to nap. She was driving because she'd slept an hour more than he had.

Alex did nap - a whole sixteen minutes of passed-out stupor with his head back on the seat till Kerri turned onto East Fourth, drove as far as Lafayette, and found a place in front of the girl's building. Fourth floor, naturally, no elevator.

No one at the P.D. was happy about declaring Sasha Perry a runaway, even though superficially it bore the signs: in her backpack she'd taken her cell phone, extra clothes and extra shoes including her cherished new Nikes. She'd been last seen shortly after nine p.m. on June second leaving her off campus apartment - but where had she gone? And why hadn't she called one friend – or her stepmother with whom she was on pretty decent terms? Every pal and acquaintance said that wasn't like her. Plus she was excited to be just days away from graduation, and addicted to texting and gabbing constantly on her cell phone. So why had her phone suddenly gone silent just hours after she was last seen?

Had she planned an overnight with some secret boyfriend? One tearful friend said that was a strong maybe. What the hell did "strong maybe" mean? Others were unaware of any boy-friend. Then a friend named Grace had a stronger suspicion that Sasha was in love but wouldn't tell who he was. That was Sasha, said Grace; if she'd been sworn to secrecy she would have enjoyed the mystery. Was he married? Grace claimed that she'd asked. Sasha had shrugged coyly and said, "Well, *taken*."

Which meant either married or in a relationship and cheating. Great. That really narrowed it down, especially since only friend Grace had said that, and then had gone back to Ohio, sad but with no further ideas. Over a hundred statements led nowhere. They had a strongly suspected homicide with no body. Resources and manpower were stretched thin and over two months had passed.

This was the end. What could they do? And if this led no-where, what could Kerri do?

10.

Door 4C opened and Becca Milstein greeted them wanly. She could have been pretty except that she was rail thin, with limp, straw-colored hair and sunken features behind wire rims.

"Hi," she said, looking downcast. "I've been re-thinking my call to you. This may be crazy. I don't know if it will help."

"Try us," Kerri said with an encouraging smile, entering the book-crammed studio. "The smallest new detail can help."

Jackets had been left in the car, which was good, because Becca's little pit wasn't air-conditioned. She had gotten used to the heat, she said as she motioned them to seats facing her African-fabric-covered daybed. Behind where she sat on the bed a small, airless window was open, but Kerri rolled her shirt sleeves higher as Alex started the questioning.

Becca explained that she was a year older than Sasha Perry – twenty-two – and that Sasha had been depressed when Becca last saw her. "When I left for Nigeria," she said softly.

"When was that?" Alex asked.

"May thirtieth. I didn't hear till weeks later that she'd disappeared two days after that. I got sick…"

Becca's eyes wandered mournfully up to her African fabric wall hangings. Then she showed them a framed photo of her with friends, grinning and hugging in some airport terminal. In the photo she was full-faced and pretty; looked maybe twenty pounds heavier. She'd only lasted nine days helping the Doctors Without Borders bunch before coming down with high fever from African tick-bite disease; no vaccine or medicine can prevent it. "Five weeks in bed," she said. "Just blotto, out of it."

When she recovered a friend in her group told her about Sasha. She had cried, but looking back her brain must have "still been shot or something" because only now was she starting to remember things. "From last spring, it seems like a million years ago."

From an Ikea storage cube covered with health drink powders and multi-vitamins she took her laptop and cell phone. Swiped at her phone, peered at a photo, then handed it to Kerri. They'd already established a rapport since it was Kerri who had taken her call; spent time talking to her.

Kerri studied Becca and Sasha Perry's selfie taken three and a half months ago. "Early May," Becca said, watching her. "When Sasha was still happy."

"When did she get depressed?" Kerri asked, handing the phone to Alex who studied the photo, then glanced back to her with a look that said, *huh?* Something seemed...off about the picture. The two friends were hugging and grinning, only Becca looked still school-year worn out and pale while Sasha's face was sunburned, her blond hair streaked lighter from being in the sun. The detectives traded looks again. Well, maybe some of them caught spring rays between classes. And sunburns fade fast; why would anyone mention a sunburn?

Becca leaned and pointed to a man, back in the shadows and barely visible behind the two young women. Alex peered more closely; enlarged the photo; handed it back to Kerri who looked and said, "Whoa."

"That guy's what I wanted you to see." Becca looked at both detectives. "It was weird. I was stressed and in a hurry, but after I told Sasha 'bye and walked away something made me look back. He'd approached her, and they *seemed* to be arguing, I can't be sure. In any case they knew each other, and there was *something* emotional going on. I'm not sure if this helps..." A helpless gesture. "Sasha knew so many people."

Kerri asked, "Does he look at all familiar?"

"No, but I'm not very observant. Usually run around like the absent-minded professor." Becca exhaled as if frustrated, troubled that she hadn't paid more attention.

Kerri leaned forward. "Back to May. Sasha seemed happy then?"

"Yes. I think she was in love from, like, maybe March to May."

Both cops traded looks, remembering: *Was he married?* friend Grace had asked Sasha. She had coyly replied, "*Well, taken.*" Until now, they'd just had that one friend's solid suspicion of a romance.

Becca just confirmed it; confirmed, in fact, a romance-gone-bad possibility.

"Any idea who the man she loved was?" Kerri asked, breathing a little faster, realizing that said mystery man wasn't necessarily the guy in the photo.

"No, she wouldn't talk about it." Becca's too-thin fingers were opening her laptop. "Something else I want to show you," she said, scrolling, then turning her Mac to face them. "This picture."

It was a photo on Facebook. Not much at first, just a pretty scene of the sun setting over the Hudson. Alex and Kerri studied it as Becca explained that Sasha had shared it to her Facebook page.

The photo was dated May second. Clearly, it was taken from the middle of the river – had to be from a boat. Kerri fast-checked something in her phone.

"That was a Saturday," she said. "To your knowledge, was Sasha friends with anyone who owned a boat?"

"No, and that's the thing." Becca pointed to the page. "See where I Liked and posted all excited?"

Under the photo was written *Wow, nice! Whose boat were you on!?* Sasha had taken the moment to Like the question - but hadn't answered. Had avoided answering.

Becca's hands suddenly flew. "Nothing like 'so-and-so or the

Smiths invited me, they're family friends.' So…when I called you I was thinking maybe her sailing friend was some guy with a jealous wife or girlfriend."

Both cops traded looks: the photo's date coincided with Sasha's brief sunburn.

They asked Becca to send her selfie with the man in the background to their phones. Kerri scribbled the Facebook's page's location; Alex hunched closer and snapped the river photo for an extra shot.

Then Kerri asked what she'd saved for last: "Did you know Sasha was questioned for forging a narcotics prescription?"

Becca hesitated, then colored. "Yes. She got caught, which most of us *don't*." She colored more deeply. "I mean, it was just for Adderall, but it got out of hand for her. She begged her doctor, said she was so tired and couldn't stay awake to study, so he prescribed a little, then she wrote over his handwriting and changed the dose. She *told* the police she was sorry."

They knew the story. Sasha had cried, promised to taper the amphetamine and never forge a prescription again. There'd been no charge. She was a struggling student, a good kid. Uppers and downers were all over, on every street corner practically; online too. What were they going to do? Arrest half the city?

They asked Becca if Sasha had gone back to using uppers. Again she colored, looked uncomfortable. "I think so."

"Just think?" from Alex.

Nod. "I got the feeling she was both depressed *and* hyper. I asked, but it was something else she wouldn't talk about. She wasn't the type to lie, so if she wouldn't talk about it…"

"You guessed she was using," Kerri said.

A sorry shrug. "She was jittery. Hyper, especially the last few times I saw her. She was trying to do so much – work, study, volunteer at the animal rescue. Her hands shook."

This was good, it was potentially very good. They'd reached

the end of their questioning, and rose and thanked, assuring Becca that she had helped, hoping she continued her recovery.

"Keep taking those vitamins," Kerri told her as they left, and Becca gave them her first smile as she closed the door.

On the stairs going down Alex said gloomily, "That guy in the selfie and whoever took Sasha on their boat – wouldn't it be nice if it were the same guy?"

Kerri groaned. Her fatigue and the heat chez Becca had caught up to her. "I know - it could be two completely different people who have nothing to do with the disappearance. *Where to take it from here?*"

Still, it was something new, tantalizing, hard not to get excited about.

Back in the car, Alex drove and Kerri sat all bunched up in the passenger seat. "New intel that might lead nowhere," she kept fretting. "It's torture."

"And they're closing the case."

"Not me. I'm staying on it if it takes forever."

"When? Our open cases need overtime and – oh jeez – there's that TV conference at four. You look exhausted. The cameras are going to think we don't let you sleep."

"Nah, I'll look ravishing."

Alex exhaled in that fretful way of his; started to ramble about cops who'd obsessed for decades over the one case that wouldn't let go. "Just don't kill yourself." He glanced worriedly over to her. "You hear me?"

Kerri didn't answer. Just stared out as he maneuvered through the heat past the Washington Square fountain again.

11.

Throw a stone in Soho and you'll hit ten bars.

Liddy chose nearby Pepe's, dim with faux-dingy nautical trappings (squint: Hemingway's Cuba), already ringing with salsa music and professionals crowding the after work scene.

She took a seat at the end of the bar under one of the burbling TVs; ordered a club sandwich and a glass of rosé. Laughing, yakking people jostled her back but she didn't turn. The wine lifted her gloom a notch, and she was aware that the bartender was trying to flirt with her. She gave him the glimmer of a smile, then some vague, friendly words as she ordered a second rosé.

She was still seeing that...whatever it was on the window's glass. The girl's face, weeping, her hair golden in the lowering sun. *She saw it, dammit!* Emerging from the droplets into woeful, begging features, then dissolving again, disappearing.

Am I losing my mind? Liddy wondered.

Pity Paul had to work late. She understood that but still wished he could be here to cheer her, make her forget and dismiss such nonsense, kibitz with the strangers behind her who wouldn't stay strangers for long - not with Paul there and everyone warmed up after a few mojitos. Paul could be charming. He could strike up conversations with anyone, crack a joke or say something clever that made them laugh, draw closer.

Liddy was the shy one, hiding behind her books and her paintings. Still, the wine was doing its job, lifting her spirits another notch, and another. She was here, in Soho! Okay, not officially moved in yet, but feeling better than she'd felt after hours alone up there in the loft's emptiness. In the mirror behind the bar she saw herself, and was surprised. Well gosh, she was even looking prettier. The sallow look was gone and her cheeks were pink, her dark eyes more alert and larger-seeming. Oh, she was feeling better, yessir. She felt ready to be friendly; nodded and said something feeling to the woman next to her complaining about her ex. She had a sudden, crazy desire to raise her glass to herself in the mirror and think, wow, the bad time's over and we're *here*, a new beginning, well done…

Abruptly the news overhead switched from a fire in midtown to the name Sasha Perry, and Liddy tensed.

A line of police officers stood behind a man in plain clothes at the microphone. Lieutenant something Mackey, grim-faced and announcing that the investigation into the disappearance of coed Sasha Perry was now officially closed, based on the assumption that she was a runaway. There had been hundreds of tips and supposed sightings with none of them panning out, he said, seeming to speak solemnly to the microphone.

"However, we still hear occasional reports, someone just re-membering something they'd previously forgotten, and I'd like to emphasize" – he looked up; said it strongly – "that one of our detectives is continuing to devote attention to this case. Detective Blasco?" He looked to the side; stepped away to make room at the mike.

She was tall, slender in a white blouse and dark blazer with dark blond hair in a ponytail, shadowed circles under her eyes. Soulful, probing eyes that scrutinized the crowd before her as if looking for bad guys.

She re-introduced herself. "Call me Kerri," she said, squinting into late day sunlight. "As Lieutenant Mackey said, I'm keeping at this. The tips and possible sightings still come – in fact, since we announced this morning that the case was closing, they've started up again. Maybe that's what police announcements do. Or *maybe* there's someone out there just remembering, just getting back to town… anything. Do we have that picture, Ray?"

She looked toward what must have been a monitor as the shot switched to a photo of Sasha Perry in her graduation picture, smiling and happy with her blond hair cut to medium-length. The photo stayed for long seconds as the detective's voice continued, then switched back to those soulful, determined eyes staring straight into the camera. "If you feel you might know something, nothing's too small. My name again is Detective Kerri Blasco, and I'm at Midtown North Precinct, 306 West 54th Street. Thank you."

Voices commented behind and around Liddy, and her bad feeling roared back.

Sasha Perry...the weeping girl's face on the window glass looked like her; ditto the girl Liddy had seen and sketched walking past them on Prince Street. Or *thought* she'd seen? Crazy, irrational nonsense! She'd fought it for the whole long hours working and measuring in the loft and she fought it now; heard Beth saying, *You're sensitive, must have seen it at the hospital...it was another trauma...*

Some compulsion made her reach to her bag, pull out her sketchbook, look at the drawing. There she was, Sasha Perry or almost her...The hair longer, the lips fuller and more serious, pursed in thought – but wait, that's because she'd passed them just walking, not smiling for her graduation picture.

"My God, that's her!" the woman next to her exclaimed, gaping at the sketch. "Those eyes, you've caught her exactly!" She'd had a few; her attention flew from the complaints she'd been making about men to the drawing. She pulled back on her stool and peered wide-eyed at Liddy. "Did you know her?"

An uneasy smile. "No, just saw her picture." *Actually she might have passed us on the street.* "I sketch people's faces a lot."

"Coulda fooled me." The woman hunched closer to study the sketch. "I took studio art. The hardest thing is showing what someone feels and you've done it! Really captured her – hey Meg, look at this!"

Meg pushed in to see and then two other women and a man, all gibbering about what a perfect likeness. "Even have her hair longer," one of them piped. "Like it would have been *after* her graduation picture. You sure you haven't seen her?"

Liddy assured them she hadn't, gathered up her things, and pushed out. Her heart thudded.

She got a cab at the corner of West Broadway. "Eighty-third and West End," she told the driver and leaned back, letting out a long, pent-up breath. The wine had worked for maybe five minutes and then - forget it. Happy Hour, what a misnomer. She felt so alone, and scared, and suddenly realized she didn't want to go home. Not right away. Paul, why do you have to be so obsessed with your work? Would it kill you to come home a little earlier? Would it kill Carl? Admit it, Paul, Carl calls the shots…he always has…

Nothing's too small, that detective said. Kerri, her name was? She seemed nice, probably wouldn't laugh at yet another crackpot story. They've gotten hundreds of tips and sightings, Liddy thought; I'd just be another one, and *maybe I'll feel better getting this off my chest.*

It was after seven. Would Detective Kerri still be there? That police conference looked taped in late afternoon.

"Ah, there's been a change?" Liddy leaned forward to the driver. "Make that 306 West 54th Street?"

The cab swerved, and she frowned. Funny, she thought, how I remembered that address. Must have planned this without realizing…

12.

Kerri Blasco stood from her desk and stretched her arms. Her shoulders and neck felt stiff, her whole body half asleep. The crib upstairs beckoned, but she was wired from too much coffee.

"You gonna go home? See if it's still there?"

Buck Dillon, last one leaving from the day shift, stopped by her desk. The squad room was mostly quiet.

Kerri exhaled and dropped back to her chair. "I'll catch a few Zs upstairs. What do I have to go home to? The cat's been fed and doesn't miss me."

Alex had tried, now it was Buck's turn to reason. He, Alex and Jo Babiak had volunteered to stay and help with the sudden uptick of new sightings. One of them was a psychic who wanted cash for her exciting new reading. Six others weren't much better. Still, no use arguing with the tired, pretty cop now mumbling back to Buck, trying to get comfortable with her arms folded and her cheek down on her laptop she was trying to use as a pillow.

He bent to her, spoke gently to the obsessed person with the squeezed-shut eyes. "Kerri, please, they've closed this one down. There's no more *funds* for it. Don't you have to worry about your cat's *future*?"

"I've set up a trust fund."

"Uh, detectives?" they heard from the door. Kerri raised her head and they both looked that way.

A uniformed man stood there with a worried-looking woman. Pretty, dark-haired, mid thirties, already looking back to the stairway they'd come up as if she'd changed her mind and wanted to flee.

"This way." The officer made her mind up for her and led her to Kerri. "Another possible sighting of Sasha Perry," he said, glancing at Buck, trying not to roll his eyes.

Kerri was up and alert again, offering a seat, welcoming the woman whose large dark eyes looked more uncertain than crazy or out for cash. She gave her name – Liddy Barron – and sat, clasped her hands, worked them against each other.

"You need me?" Buck asked after giving the newcomer the once-over, glancing hopefully for the door.

"No thanks, we're good." The two men left, looking relieved, and Kerri gave Liddy a friendly smile.

"So," she said, opening her laptop and starting a new file. "You may have seen Sasha Perry?"

Liddy's hands flew apart. "*Big* may. I may also be losing my mind."

Kerri couldn't help it – she laughed. "Welcome to my world," she said, and watched the woman facing her untense a little; appreciate the shared moment of irony. Honesty up front, how different.

"And where do you think you saw Sasha?"

"On Prince Street last Sunday," Liddy blurted fast to outrace losing her nerve. Then fell back in her chair, peered dubiously back to Kerri. "I'm waiting for you to laugh again."

"Not at all." Kerri smiled but said nothing, letting her silence prod.

Liddy breathed in. "I was with my husband and a friend at Gino's sidewalk café. They were yakking and I was half listening, sketching people walking past. I'm an artist, and one of the people I sketched was, well…"

She reached and got out her sketchbook. Opened shakily to the page. Leaned to put the book open on Kerri's desk, angling it to show her. "This girl."

Kerri looked. Brought her face closer, blinking, then raised her eyes back to Liddy.

"I thought it was just another sketch," Liddy said, still nervous. "Didn't place the face at all. My friend Beth kept saying, 'She *reminds* me of someone,' but couldn't remember who, and I forgot it till Beth called me today and insisted, 'It's her, that missing coed.'"

Kerri still stared at the sketch, frowning a little. "You didn't place the face? This girl's photo was in the news for over a week."

"Coinciding with me being in the hospital. I was in an accident. Got, uh, run over, had a broken leg, two cracked ribs and a concussion." Liddy clasped her hands again and looked down at them, clearly pained. When she looked back the detective's eyes bore the intensity that had stared through the camera at the police conference.

"So I never saw those news reports. Never saw this girl's face, though it's been suggested to me that someone may have turned on the news in my hospital room as I started to get better. I don't know. I don't remember." Liddy's voice trembled. "From the concussion, there's a *lot* I don't remember."

Kerri was tapping keys on her laptop. "Gino's is at 110b Prince Street."

"Right. A few doors down and across the street from the loft we just bought. We hadn't seen it yet, actually. My friend Beth is a realtor and tried to talk us out of it."

"Oh? Why was that?" Kerri was getting a funny feeling. The sketch and this story... She watched Liddy Barron hesitate, clearly pained.

"Because of what I'd been through...and because it's the apartment where the actor Charlie Bass hung himself." Liddy winced as she said it.

"I know that case. Very sad. He had promise, talent."

The two were silent for a moment. Kerri's gaze was back on the sketch. The resemblance was eerie; the eyes looked right back at her. But the most striking thing...

Kerri tapped the sketch. "You've drawn a stud in her ear."

Liddy leaned and looked; nodded. "Right. A funny-shaped stud high in her right ear. Maybe a rounded daisy shape?"

"You saw her wearing that?"

"I must have, that's what I sketched. Now I don't exactly remember." Liddy blinked; frowned a little. "Wait – I do remember, yes, it was an irregular rounded shape."

Kerri held her breath. "That's interesting, because Sasha didn't wear that stud in her graduation picture. I don't think it was in any of the photos released to the press."

Liddy looked at the detective, surprised.

"Think hard," Kerri urged, leaning an elbow on her desk to steady herself. Her heart pounded. "In your mind can you remember, a little more closely, what that stud looked like? You said it was rounded…"

"Yes, but not *one* rounded shape." Liddy's brow creased; she shook her head a little. "More like a small round on top of a bigger round…kind of like a snowman or…or – I've *got* it," she cried, and pointed to the sketch. "It was a teddy bear!"

13.

Shut it down, say no more, Kerri thought though she was bursting, just exploding to take it further. Liddy Barron had come close but there was more, something incredibly specific, to this tiny detail never released to the press. Kerri couldn't say what but her mind raced, trying to figure this. Sasha had loved that stud but hadn't worn it a lot – although, oddly, she wore it the night she disappeared; two friends had seen her, kidded her about it.

Just two friends but still…others had seen it other times; the description could have traveled - but to this Liddy Barron? Not part of the university scene?

Slow, Kerri decided, controlling her breathing. Get a fix on this. Ask more.

"Do you remember what else this girl was wearing?"

Liddy's finger was on her sketch, tapping lightly on the little stud she'd almost just identified; had only depicted in a quick, charcoal blur. "Just that pale T-shirt," she said vaguely, looking frustrated. "I don't remember what color it was."

She looked up. "Was I right about the teddy bear?"

Kerri smiled. "Close. Very close."

"But not exact?"

"Not exact."

Liddy felt defeated. Well, she'd been a good citizen, done all she could. She looked away and felt her heart speed up, wanting to say more but it would sound crazy. This was the most she could offer - a possible sighting, an address, and a not really identified piece of jewelry. She gave a regretful shrug; reached for her purse. "I'm sorry, that's all I've got. It's not much is it?"

Kerri's eyes probed this woman who suddenly looked torn; just sat in a conflicted-looking heap holding her purse limply. Her sketchbook lay forgotten on the desk.

"There's more, isn't there?" Kerri asked quietly, leaning forward. "Something else you want to tell me?"

Liddy rose; shook her head no but slowly, as if in turmoil. "That's it, I'm afraid." She picked up her sketchbook and started to move; hesitated; then turned with tight-lipped capitulation on her face.

"Have I seemed sane to you so far?"

"Yes." Kerri smiled, her eyes soft.

The compulsion was building, building. Liddy's heart beat hard and she couldn't stand it another second. "Well, here's where you will think me nuts because…" Her words tumbled. "I've been seeing this girl…Sasha…even before I knew who she was. I've seen her in…crazy places, where mist condenses especially, like on the shower stall glass, or three hours ago on the window glass next to plants I sprayed."

Ping!

A white, bright light went off in Kerri's head, which was odd, because what her police mind should have thought was, Okay, yeah, crazy. Hallucinating, seeing what isn't there. But the water connection did it, made her think this might really be something. If they hadn't been to Becca Milstein's earlier…

She patted the chair Liddy had just left. "Sit," she said gently, and Liddy did; looked relieved and dropped down again, slump-shouldered.

"The shower stall and plants?" Kerri prodded.

"I said I was crazy."

"Crazy people don't say they're crazy. Tell me."

Liddy gulped air and described because she wanted to, desperately. "Four days ago I thought I saw a girl's face in the mist on the shower glass; then today I saw the face again, next to these huge plants that were Charlie Bass's. They're close to a big window that faces south, and the sun practically fries them so they need to be sprayed..." She exhaled hard. "See? Crazy."

"Did the face appear before you sprayed the plants?"

"No. After. And today was more frightening because the sun was angling in just right to make the hair seem blond – well, the whole face glowed and seemed to be weeping, begging...you know, how condensation coalesces and then seems to cry down tears? I was freaked and staring at it just as my friend Beth called."

"Did you tell her?"

"No. Don't want her or my husband to worry, they've been through enough with my accident - from which I still haven't exactly recovered." A tear stung and Liddy wiped it. "I forget things, can't remember..."

"Have you ever seen other things? Visions?"

"God no! Never. Beth is convinced I made Sasha Perry's sketch from memory 'cause I'd seen it in the hospital, internalized it because it too was a trauma." Liddy wiped her other eye almost angrily. Clearly felt embarrassed.

Subtly, Kerri tapped her index finger in thought. Something was coming together for her. *Maybe*, she thought, and leaned forward, heeding a hunch.

"The shower and the plants," she said, locking gazes with Liddy. "Both involve water."

"I guess."

"Do you swim? Do water sports?"

Liddy seemed surprised. "Yes. I was on a swimming team as a kid, and my husband has a boat."

"Here in New York?"

"Yes. Docked at the 79th Street Boat Basin. We haven't been able to use it because of my accident – that was on June 3rd. And we didn't use it much before that this year because my husband works long hours, and now it's for sale because we're shifting finances." Liddy's face worried. "You think water's some kind of connection?"

"Could be. When people experience trauma it's the familiar things that go kablooey." Kerri watched Liddy's reaction to that; seem to find a little comfort. Then she asked, casually, "What's your husband's name, by the way? What does he do?"

Those dark eyes looked worn out, unguarded. "Paul Barron and he's a neuroscientist. Researches and teaches at NYU. Mostly researches now." Liddy seemed to re-think something and gave a start, leaned forward urgently.

"I'd die if he knew I came here."

"He won't."

"He's pure logic, thinks I'm *too* creative. We're so different - I'm visual, he just sees facts. These crazy visions I've told you...if he heard about it-"

"He won't." Kerri reached and gave Liddy her card. "It was good of you to come. Please call if there's anything else. I'd also like to call you if that's alright."

Liddy nodded and gave her cell phone number. Kerri thanked; smiled gently. "Do you have medications to help you?"

Liddy stood, gathered up her things. "Yes. Mild tranquilizers and a nice shrink who's helping me through my whatever-it-is. PTSD, sort of, with a dash of amnesia." She looked pained again; inhaled. "I thought coming here would help. Get this off my chest."

"Has it helped?" Kerri rose and held out her hand.

"I don't know." Liddy shook wearily, mumbled a jumble of thanks, and left.

14.

It didn't help.

The apartment seemed oppressive, claustrophobic. The *old* apartment was how Liddy now thought of it, turning on a lamp. Filled Bekins boxes ready for the movers crammed the living room. She kicked one of them. Out popped one of Paul's tennis balls, bonking and clunking across the floor, a weird, echoing sound. She wove through more boxes and so much *stuff* – antiques and curios they'd collected now crowding the room. She lit another lamp, but the room was still full of shadows. After Soho, so silent.

At least it smelled of turpentine, which meant home to her, although soon, soon, a real studio with a real north light. The thought lifted her spirits a bit.

By the window was her "temporary studio." That's what Paul called it, trying to cheer her when he hauled her easel and draftsman's table and art supplies from the studio she'd been renting. He'd set her up next to the small, drab window which at least faced north, but overlooked the back of another apartment building. Under the easel and the rest he'd spread a tan tarp to protect the – ugh – ugly, wall-to-wall beige carpet that had been there since before he first took the apartment. "What bachelor redecorates?" he'd joked the first time Liddy saw the place.

She surveyed her about-to-be-old work area, thinking how pinched it looked. Then she looked at her current painting, drying on its easel.

It looked good. She'd worked on it the last three days, thrilled after they decided on the loft, and her excitement showed in her brushwork, the bright swoops and stabs of color pulled across the handsome warrior's tense, high cheekbone. Rawlie, his name was apparently - brave space warrior fighting attacking aliens and simultaneously protecting beautiful princess Whatsername, tucked fearfully behind him in breast-revealing flowing fabric. Ha, see that? Even in the post-apocalyptic future it's gotta be the guy protecting the girl dressed scantily even in raging battle, but the author was male and that's the cover the publisher wanted, so that was that.

Liddy sat on her stool before the painting, contemplating now her wide palette busy-bright with blobs of squeezed-out pigment. There was even more energy still in her brushwork on the palette itself - dabbing, mixing, smearing till the new hue was just right, waiting to be hoisted up on the eager brush.

Liddy sighed.

The loft had energized her for three days. Even sleep had been better the last three nights, with no frightening dreams or visions re-appearing until…

Today. Thursday. That apparition glowing before Charlie Bass's plants. Hours had passed and Liddy still saw the girl, young and blond, weeping on the glass; still felt that sense of cold shock. And that visit to the police! The surprise that the detective was most interested in Sasha Perry's ear stud - which Liddy had seen and drawn and now couldn't remember.

"Was I right about the teddy bear?" she asked.

"Close. Very close," Detective Kerri Blasco smiled and said.

How the bleep close can you be to guessing a teddy bear and not have it *be* a teddy bear? It bothered Liddy; bothered her a lot because maybe remembering could help? Make the visions stop?

She shuddered. Stormed at herself to get normal again. Happier times ahead!

She moved off the stool, which she'd been using because her leg still hurt, and turned on the Tensor light over her draftsman table where she did her watercolors. She'd been rushing the Rawlie painting, working simultaneously on another job which called for an elaborate, scary watercolor of a woman fleeing terror in the rain. Jobs had piled up during her convalescence. Great, now there'd be the pressure of the move *and* catching up, and the fear of that poor girl's face coming back...

Stop it, fight it! she stormed again, rubbing goose bumps on her arms, going into the kitchen.

Eight-thirty read the glowing red digits on the microwave. Liddy turned on the light over the counter and realized she was hungry. Pulled something in a box out of the freezer, shoved it into the microwave, sat and waited the three minutes while the magic motor whirred its low, rumbling song and then went *Ding!*

"Oh!" she jumped, felt her heart leap. So tense, she thought, gotta calm-

And her phone buzzed. She answered, gasping.

"Where's the fire?" Paul, sounding worried.

"The microwave scared me."

Silence. "My fault. You're alone too much nights. So if the damned thing just went off it means you haven't eaten yet, right?"

"Right."

"Am I interrupting anything gourmet and delicious?"

"Dunno, didn't look at the box."

He laughed. "Then I'm just in time because I'm done for the day. Want to go out? Romantic dinner at Chez Pierre's?"

"Be still my heart."

"I'm leaving now. Be home in ten minutes barring traffic. Just think, soon - walking distance!"

15.

She washed up and put on lipstick. In the bedroom changed into a white, belted tunic over her black jeans. Wandered the living room again while she waited.

After they married she'd prettied up the place as best she could, but the Recession had hit; her book-cover jobs ran dry and the research grant of Paul working alone was cancelled. So sorry, hard times, said the University and the Big Pharma firm that had wanted to partner. Four hard years followed; then suddenly things were better. Liddy found her work more in demand than she'd dreamed possible - and fifteen months ago, after Paul had moaned to Carl about losing his grant, a new grant with Paul and Carl researching together for better speed was re-instated, big time, with lots of excitement and heavy-hitting science and business types all hopped up waiting to hear their presentation in five weeks.

What, really, had made that grant finally happen? Liddy had often wondered about that. Was it Carl's family pull with Big Pharma, or better times, or the fact that Carl's idea for their research was slightly better? Paul said it was the latter two, which probably made sense although he'd been toiling alone on something similar; would no doubt have come up with the same damned thing if the wheels hadn't started turning again so fast.

Liddy leaned on the door jamb, surveying the living room, realizing that she was saying good-bye to a big chunk of her life. It was almost funny how they'd jam-packed so much *stuff* in here, knowing that they'd move someday and that this place was just a temporary warehouse. They'd prowled antique and curio shops.

Found a wonderful old Spanish armoire which they'd cleared of dust and cobwebs and made beautiful again. Ditto an old walnut desk, a big Spanish terra cotta jar, and a fat Buddha that was just a copy and did nothing but take up space. "Floor crowders," Paul called them, but Liddy had loved them; still did.

She felt herself give way to a smile, realizing that the things jamming this old place would almost be lost in the loft; have more than enough room to spread out in and be beautiful. She toyed with the idea of maybe a small spotlight beaming on the Buddha, maybe even asking the construction guys to build a niche for him, off to the right of the fireplace and the television…

Keys scraped at the door and there was Paul, filling the room with his energy and a fierce hug and lusty kiss. He changed his shirt and, despite a soft rain starting to fall, out they went to their favorite little French restaurant on Amsterdam and 86th. From their table by the window, he looked wistfully out at the street.

"Last time we'll be here," he said smiling, raising his Beaujolais to Liddy's glass.

"Maybe we'll come back," she shrugged, but Paul didn't think so.

"You kidding? It's a whole different world in Soho. A really new beginning."

Between wine and poulet rôti they checked their phones to track delivery of new cookware and a new, king-sized bed they'd ordered. The wine warmed as Liddy described mundane things like the construction company who was going to come work extra fast ("maybe tomorrow") because Beth sent them so much business; ditto the fabric firm Beth sent tons of business who were going to re-do fast the couch and ottoman and also help Liddy hang drapes and window shades. "A blessing," she said. "I'd go crazy if I had to take that time away from painting."

"Money sure talks," Paul said, dumping salt onto his pommes frites.

Under the mundane, though, Liddy's trip to the police station troubled her – rather, what really bothered was feeling that she shouldn't or couldn't tell Paul. *Why not?* her mind rebelled. I'll just say I thought I saw and sketched that missing coed, and told the police where. Shouldn't married people be able to share confidences? Not feel afraid to say whatever especially if it upsets them?

She found herself staring at the little red squares in the red-and-white-checked tablecloth. Her fingertips touched them; moved across a jagged line of them. Forget the police visit.

It bothered her worse after their second glass of wine, over a dessert of shared tarte aux pommes and vanilla ice cream with fresh strawberries sprinkled on top. She stopped eating for moments; stared at the red strawberries. Say nothing about the police.

It bothered her still worse as they nursed two brandies - an extra celebration, a saying good-bye to the old neighborhood. Liddy caught herself staring at a woman at a near table wearing a red sweater. It was the sweater she stared at – and then thought, *why am I staring at red things?*

"You know her?" Paul asked.

"No. Just admiring her sweater."

She slugged her brandy too fast, let it take effect, and out it came.

She told Paul, casually, as if it were nothing: she was just the thousandth person reporting a possible sighting of that missing girl, a good citizen doing her civic duty.

Paul looked at her as if he hadn't heard right. "You're kidding."

"No."

"God, stay away from the police."

"Why? If I or anybody can help-"

"Just don't get involved, any lawyer will tell you that. Don't even give them the time of day, they'll find noon at three o'clock."

He frowned uneasily as something hit. "Had you been drinking before you went there?"

Furious, the question made her, but she hid it and shrugged. "I just stopped at Pepe's."

"Where?"

"A bar on Prince. I had some wine."

"How *much* wine? Jesus, Lids, I thought you were better handling-"

"Two glasses. *Nothing*, for God's sake."

"Please don't tell me *that* problem's coming back."

"*It was never a problem*. I had two glasses and stopped fine. The detective said they had a hundred new sightings. She was nice."

"Detective," Paul muttered, rolling his eyes away as if she'd just falsely announced the place was on fire. With his hand holding his brandy he signaled the waiter, sloshing the brandy.

Liddy clamped her jaw; looked out. Say no more, she warned herself. When they fought, they really fought.

The rain outside was heavier, fogging up the glass. There was no scary face on it, though. She looked, and then looked harder.

Nothing. But she still felt rotten.

16.

The man in the shadows…

He was standing under a tree, chin lowered with darkened eyes clearly watching. Looked as if he'd just stood from that bench behind him, watching Sasha and Becca.

Waiting for Becca to leave?

Looked it.

Kerri went back to studying the selfie – enlarged - of Becca and Sasha taken three and a half months ago. *"Early May,"* Becca said. *"When Sasha was still happy."*

ShadowFace's features were too lost in the shadows, dammit.

After I told Sasha 'bye and walked away something made me look back. He'd approached her, they seemed to be arguing, I'm not sure. There was something emotional going on.

Becca thought Sasha had been in love from roughly March through May. Then was depressed by May thirtieth, the last time Becca saw her. And Becca was the second person (!) to think there might have been a romance gone bad.

Kerri went back to her computer and zoomed through files, to the interview done last June by a different detective. She found it: Grace now back in Ohio had suspected a lover and asked Sasha if he was married. "Taken," was the coy answer. That interview had just gotten filed away, lost in the cracks because Grace had been the only one to strongly suspect a romance.

And the idea of a romance gone bad? That hadn't come up at all.

Until today.

Becca.

Excruciating new possibilities.

Kerri had flagged Liddy Barron's file the second she left. Into that new file Kerri copied the Grace interview, Becca's interview with her matching observations, and the enlarged selfie of Becca and Sasha with ShadowFace in the background.

She fell back in her chair, tired to the point of seeing double, unwilling to give it a rest.

The body language of photos was something Kerri believed in strongly, and Becca's selfie alone was a breakthrough. It wasn't much but it put up a big red flag to any thought of sleep. Kerri had already put ShadowFace through facial recognition software, had expected nothing and gotten nothing - just dizzy watching the faces zoom past: *perp* faces - not faces like the selfie's well-built guy in a polo shirt and blazer, his type more likely to be a high-class swindler than a stalker.

Kerri switched her thoughts back to Liddy Barron.

A bizarre story, but still... The eerie water connection combined with Becca's photo of the Hudson – correction - Sasha's photo of the Hudson, clearly taken in the middle of the river from a boat, then shared to Becca's Facebook page.

See where I Liked and posted all excited? Wow, nice! Whose boat were you on!?

Sasha had taken the moment to like the question - but had avoided answering. And Becca told them, "*I started thinking it was maybe some guy with a jealous wife or girlfriend.*"

Oh boy. It was all copied into the Liddy Barron file.

From the hall, sounds of feet pounding up the stairs then two night detectives rushed in, one with blood on his shirt. He grimaced hi and headed upstairs, to the showers and the crib. The other gave a wave, inquired about Kerri's cat ("still climbing up your curtains?"), and started notes at his desk.

Kerri made a fist and gnawed on her thumb a little; went back to trying to connect things.

Alex had pinpointed where Sasha's photo was taken: the river off 89th or 90th Street. He'd recognized the Jersey side; that spot was up just a bit from the 79th Street Boat Basin.

Where Liddy Barron with her water obsession said they docked their boat.

The police knew the Boat Basin well. From late April through October it bustled with tourists taking pictures, weekend sailors crowding the docks for an afternoon sail, parties going on days and nights with the boats still moored. There had been drownings there, too, usually alcohol-related and accidental, but not till proven otherwise.

A very popular place.

Her headache was blasting, so Kerri lay her head down on her desk and closed her eyes. Dammit, three hours ago her excitement had surged for the first time in weeks. Now what? The desk top was cool, at least; really a nice place to help the head and kinda like an ice pack when you got right down to it; just float with your eyes closed and stop trying to think at warp speed; let the thoughts just come…

Problem…big problem: were ShadowFace in the selfie and whoever took Sasha on their boat *even the same person?* Who knew? More to the point - what if they *were* the same person?

Circumstantial! Prove a connection to the disappearance!

Could Sasha Perry have wandered over and flirted with some boat owner? Been invited for a sail and never come home?

Kerri groaned, louder than she'd intended. The night detective who'd inquired about her cat looked over. "You just blow a fuse?"

She opened her eyes. "Yup."

"You should try real sleeping once in a while, seriously."

"It's overrated."

"So why are you moaning? Go upstairs. Lie down. Leave a note for room service."

"Ha, you're a riot." Kerri watched him go back to his notes, closed her eyes again.

Umm, no…Sasha didn't seem the type to flirt with strangers, and she'd left her apartment with just enough for an overnight - there was little missing from her room - which suggested she felt comfortable headed to someone she knew.

Someone she knew…*yes.*

Kerri sat up again and went back to Liddy Barron's file.

Her laptop keys clicked as she googled *Paul Barron, neuroscience*…and there he was, lots of pictures. Good-looking, dark-haired with another dark-haired guy in one picture, both of them fifteen months ago in black tie and tux, smiling at some big science shindig.

"…recipients of the coveted Baker-Renolfi Pharmaceuticals grant for advanced anesthesia research," said the caption, naming the man next to Barron as Carl Finn, NYU adjunct professor of human biology, M.D., PhD in neuroscience like Paul Barron…

Kerri blinked; stared at the screen.

Both men taught where Sasha Perry had been a student. Not just the university, but in the same department.

And the other guy Carl Finn was also an M.D.?

What they'd asked Becca flashed through Kerri's mind: *"Did you know Sasha was questioned for forging a narcotics prescription?"*

Becca had known, seemed almost to feel it was no big deal, everybody did it. Sasha had promised never again to the cops, but – forget that. Once they found how easy it was, most of them went back to needing/wanting their uppers and then downers to come down from the uppers - and Sasha was a study all night kind of girl.

And only M.D.s could prescribe narcotics! Okay…legally, though people got their drugs everywhere these days, not even counting online.

Kerri stared at the photo of the two men at the science thing, realizing that Carl Finn looked a little like the guy in the selfie.

Close but not...wait... ShadowFace last May was thinner. Carl Finn grinning in his tux was a bit heavier, fuller-faced.

But fifteen months! People lost or gained weight all the time, and ShadowFace had his chin down – as if belatedly realizing Becca was taking her pic with Sasha and *he didn't want to be in it.*

Why?

Professional as well as personal threat? Kerri again heard Becca say, "...*maybe some guy with a jealous wife or girlfriend.*"

If Sasha had continued somehow getting her uppers, she might have been wary of the types who peddled narcotics even on campus; wary too of getting it online and possibly contaminated.

More likely she'd seek out another M.D.

Kerri went onto the U's website to read more about Carl Finn. Smart guy, he had a PhD plus an M.D. - got it from a good med school, then took the all-important year of residency and passed his medical boards – without which he wouldn't be qualified to use his medical degree or prescribe drugs - and then he dropped out of medicine. Switched to the post-doc program in neuroscience.

And he was on Facebook! With friends, oh lots of friends and good times and...women. One appeared lots with his arm around her...a hard-looking blonde, mid thirties named – Kerri tag-searched her – Terri Lynde, hotshot corporate lawyer, no doubt a really big earner. Photos adoring her stopped abruptly in May. Whatsamatter, did the hard-working, has-to-teach-too researcher lose his hold on Lady Big Bucks?

Becca's voice again: "*I started thinking it was maybe some guy with a jealous wife or girlfriend.*"

Scroll, scroll...more Carl Finn photos...then Kerri's fingers stilled.

There he was, whooping it up with Paul Barron and some third guy in front of a docked sailboat. Could that be Barron's boat? There was something familiar about the third guy, behind sunglasses with his dark hair messed, but the headache throbbed and Kerri was seeing double and her attention was on Finn.

In her mind she added weight to ShadowFace and decided yes, that could be him - which still left everything circumstantial - plus it wasn't him it was Paul Barron who owned a boat, there was nothing in Facebook about Carl Finn owning a boat...oh dammit, dammit...

17.

She couldn't breathe. Her chest heaved and her arms flailed but no use, she was going down, seeing air bubbles escape from her nose. The blue circle of sky above was getting smaller. She saw the boat's hull on the surface and Paul's legs kicking away from her, swimming back up. Don't go! Then a hand touched her shoulder. She rolled in the murk clutching her soaking red teddy bear and saw Sasha, her hair swimming around her face as she wept, couldn't be comforted by the red teddy bear as she took it, and was swept away.

Liddy jerked awake, trembling, feeling Paul holding her.

"…a dream, Lids. Just a dream…"

Her hands went to her face as her heart throbbed, felt like something was crushing it. "I was drowning and you were swimming away," she breathed. "Just…leaving me."

"Because of last night." He held her tighter. "I'm sorry, I'm so sorry."

His hair was wet, must have just turned off the shower. Last night came back…

They had fought more when they got back, then had gone all silent and sullen and gone to bed mad. He conked right out, of course – he always did. Liddy had lain awake miserable, then had dropped into an uneasy sleep. Twice she'd jerked awake trembling, seen the clock at three and five-thirty, didn't remember closing her eyes again. Then the dream.

She was still seeing Sasha and…a red teddy bear? Where had that come from?

Paul had her sitting up now, his soft, urgent voice just a

drumming white noise still emitting sorry, oh Lids, I'm a turd, we've been through such pressure and that was *before* the accident. He was drying her tears with the belt of his terry robe. "The bad feeling will dissipate. Hey," he urged sweetly, "we move in four days, it's exciting! Get cracking, you'll be so busy today you'll barely have time to fit in Alex."

Who? Oh. Nooo...was it Friday already?

Alex Minton, dear shrink who'd said she was getting so much better. "Four o'clock appointment," Liddy muttered, feeling her cold dread deepen.

"Don't cancel." Paul brushed her hair from her brow. "You surfacing? Bogeyman dream leaving?"

"Yeah," she croaked, but it wasn't. She still saw the red teddy bear and couldn't understand it; managed to force a smile as he squeezed her, and then pulled back with his eyes almost beseeching. "God," he said. "I so want all of this behind us, a whole new, wonderful start."

"Wish granted." She smiled again, this time more gamely, raised her hand and waved an imaginary wand above their heads.

Paul finished dressing, kissed her again as she still lay conked under the covers, and left.

A red teddy bear? Where in God's name...?

She let her mind wander, back to the sad place and time when she was growing up. A shabby, depressed household, sickness, alcoholism, everyone too overwhelmed to pay much attention to each other, but when still young Liddy had found escape in books, read voraciously, lived in her books which were her safe place - except for one that had broken her heart. She'd even blocked out the title; now rooted in her still foggy mind, and back it came. *The Red Pony*, by...more rooting, and the author's name came: John Steinbeck. Fifteen, had she been when she read it? And cried for days. Vowed never to forgive that terrible man Steinbeck for having written something so sad.

But she'd never forgotten the book, not really. Like a scar that's an unavoidable part of growing up, it had always stayed with her, under the surface but still there, a big emotional scar that, in retrospect, was a lesson in life.

So?

Red pony, red teddy bear? Did that make sense?

Her visit to Kerri Blasco came back too, and not being able to quite identify that ear stud of Sasha's. *How close can you be to guessing a teddy bear and not have it be a teddy bear?*

She couldn't figure any of it. Let her mind continue to fret it as she finally got up and got busy, emitting a groan, thinking how much there was to do.

An hour later she was filling and labeling more Bekins boxes, still feeling a tightness in her chest but using minutiae to push it down. Beth called to say the construction people were already at the loft, she let them in, then had to run up to East 76th.

"Wow, fast."

"They're in the neighborhood finishing a different job, happy to segue right into yours. They're fast, by the way, can fix a floor or put up a wall in a day. So girlfriend, how are you doing?"

For a second too long Liddy said nothing, and Beth groaned. "Not another nightmare?"

"'Fraid so. Hell waking up, but it's dissipating."

"Oh Lids."

"Maybe when I get crazy busy, back on track…"

Beth groaned again. "Let's hope." At the other end someone called to her. "Speaking of crazy busy, I may have screwed up sending everybody to the loft at once. It sounds like the construction people are getting under each other's feet."

"Who do I call? What are their names?"

Beth told her. "Oh, and Henry the lock and alarm guy? He's waiting for you to call about changing your security system." She gave that number too.

"I'll call."

"Love ya, sweetie. Call if you don't feel good."

Liddy hung up; sighed. Wished again she could have told Beth about the blond girl's apparition on the window, and her visit to the police to show her sketch, and Paul's pique about that...but she couldn't. Beth would fret, say you shouldn't have taken the loft, blame herself for showing it to them in the first place.

Just hang in there, Liddy told herself, and paced, punching numbers on her phone.

Frankie the Sheetrock guy complained that the Con Ed guy shouldn't be there yet, he was in the way. She handled it, then talked to the painter confused about his paint chips, and the plumber complaining about the electrician updating the kitchen center island - she had a hard time understanding, the plumber seemed to be speaking mostly Ukrainian - but she handled it.

Shortly after one she went for what was probably her last trip to the local supermarket, where she found herself staring at the red tomatoes. She didn't need tomatoes, but stood there like a dummy staring at them; had to wrench herself away. Then picked up a few more things and found herself staring at a red cereal box. A ridiculous product, all sugar and fake color and really unhealthy – something they'd never touch – so why was she suddenly holding it in her hand gazing at it? She caught herself, put it back, got a few more things and got out.

Was back at the old place busy unpacking when a FedEx package came – café curtains, which she unwrapped and put in a packing box with towels and linens. Then in the bedroom she emptied more drawers and put their contents into boxes, stopping to hold up an old red T-shirt, stare at it...

...and suddenly it was 3:30.

Already? No... Dread time again.

In the bathroom she stopped brushing her hair, took a breath, and peered into the shower stall still misted from their showers.

No young girl's face in residence on the walls; there hadn't been one earlier when she showered either, thank goodness. This morning's dream was quite enough, the red teddy bear still swirled in the blue current of her dream. It troubled her bad, wouldn't go away.

She picked up her brush again. In the mirror, suddenly, like a flash or a dream, she saw Sasha reach to her through the water, and sadly take the teddy bear. Liddy blinked; blinked hard as she saw them both sweep away in the current.

The heart rocketed, the heart, the heart...

She put her brush down; leaned both hands on the sink. Accept it, she told herself, fighting tears. They've been there all along: the frightening images, the slow banging of the heart, the constricted feeling in the chest. They ease off a bit when the hands are busy, roar back when they're not, but they're always there, waiting. You can hide from anything but your mind.

She went back to the bedroom, got out that red T-shirt again, held it too long with her hands trembling.

Then checked the time, grabbed her purse, and ran out slamming the door. The hallway echoed the slam. The elevator had a little girl in it, who gripped her mother's hand tighter and stared at Liddy, round-eyed. The child had her obsessing about teddy bears. The mother noticed, and asked kindly, "Are you alright?"

"I'm fine, thanks!" Liddy said too loudly.

In the lobby she realized she'd forgotten to lock up. Took the damned elevator back up, re-opened the door, set the slide bolt to snap closed, then keyed home the second lock.

Her hands shook worse.

I'm a total mess, she thought, signaling for a cab.

18.

Alex Minton frowned for a second time. "On the glass?" he said. "You saw the face on the glass?"

"Yes, after I sprayed." Liddy hated the tremor in her voice. "And on the misted shower stall before that, both since my last visit. Then this morning the dream."

He looked like he'd stepped out of a Maurice Sendak story, built like a soft-bodied bear, with glasses that made his face look like an owl and a short, trimmed beard. Now he took off his glasses and started wiping them, which was a bad sign; it meant he'd just heard something he couldn't figure.

"You said your nightmares were lessening," he said, looking up again.

"I said they were getting further apart, but when they do happen they're more upsetting." Liddy clamped her lips together, then exhaled in a rush. "The apparitions and my sketch resemble that missing girl Sasha Perry. It's like I'm seeing a ghost."

Minton scribbled a note. *What?* Give her more pills? His note taking was something else Liddy noticed he did when he seemed at a loss for pronouncements. She'd laid it all out for him, emphasizing her friend's idea that maybe she'd seen Sasha's picture on the news in her hospital room; remembered it subconsciously because it was another trauma.

"Could that be it, do you think?" Liddy leaned forward.

Minton raised his eyebrows a little. "Very possibly," he said. "In fact, I think you've identified what we shrinks call the 'diversion cause' - which, plainly put, is something that is actually easier for the psyche to deal with than the real issue." He stopped to think for a moment. "Some repressed memories are so terrifying that one is unable to remember, let alone face. The work you must do going forward is, first, identify the real root cause, and second, deal with that."

"I think the real root cause is the fact that I got run over and my head creamed and only recently remembered where my sock drawer is." Liddy felt her jaw muscles tighten.

Minton chuckled indulgently, made another note. It occurred to Liddy that until this latest, long pronouncement of his she'd been doing most of the talking. He'd stated a generalization – great – but he didn't know what to do with her. She'd heard of people going twenty years to a psychiatrist and getting nowhere.

The red teddy bear he thought was "possibly" a hopeful sign: a comfort toy bringing the psyche back to a safe place. But why a *red* teddy bear? Again, he thought, it might connect with that Steinbeck story – and she really did love it, didn't she? That's why she never forgot it, another re-connecting with childhood self-comfort.

"But why would the red teddy bear be *wet*?" Liddy pressed, getting frustrated. "Soaking wet under water?"

Minton frowned and wrote a note; then took a long time wiping his glasses. "Perhaps we should discuss that on our next visit."

Liddy stared down at her hands.

He inquired – as he had every last time - if her husband was still being supportive.

Yes, very.

And was the marriage good?

Yes, she answered, as she had before.

"Most important, has your husband-"

"Paul."

"Ah yes. Has Paul helped you remember what, exactly, *happened* on the night of the accident? *How* it happened? What caused you to run out like that?"

Dammit, he'd asked that each time too – emphasizing the

same words. Each time she'd answered as best she could and now suddenly felt annoyed; these sessions were starting to sound like the same script read over and over. Okay, she told herself, he was trying to see if there was any update, anything further that either she or Paul remembered.

Liddy clasped her hands together, hard, wanting to crack her knuckles or something. "Same as what you've already got. We'd been drinking, and we fought. Mainly, Paul says, I was upset because he was so obsessed with his work, always getting home late, and I felt neglected."

"That's what Paul says?"

"Yes and it was true. Still is although he's better, he's been coming home a bit earlier these days – nights, rather - despite being under the gun for a research project deadline."

"Had you fought about his work obsession before?"

"I had complained, but…well, respected what he's doing. It will be a big breakthrough if they can pull this off."

"Ah yes, you mentioned he has a research partner."

Liddy shrugged yes. Anticipated the next question and beat him to it. "Did I holler he spent more time with his partner than he did with me? Probably. I don't remember."

"Because you'd been drinking."

"That night we'd *both* been drinking – me even more, Paul says. He barely remembers all the details. Mainly he says I screamed 'I've had it!' and ran out. I have no memory of going down in the elevator or running through the lobby, and I can't believe I had any intention of getting run over - or even being in the street. Maybe I'd just thought of storming down the sidewalk or something."

Liddy stopped for breath, watching Minton write again.

What was he writing? He had it already - they'd both been blotto and fought and neither could remember that night because they'd fried their brains. Minton had it already!

And the fifty minutes were almost up. Minton glanced surreptitiously at his watch. Now, went the script, he would quickly ask the other stuff.

Her painting, was she able to work and concentrate?

"Yes."

"Is the move causing increased pressure? Perhaps that's why you've been having these…experiences."

"I don't mind if you call them hallucinations. But they started, remember, before we saw the loft. The face in the shower stall."

"That was the day you were to go looking."

"True, but the nightmares started way before that, which is why I came to you in the first place. As for the move and pressure, there's some – but after the disruption I can't wait to get back to painting full time."

"You're bursting to push your brush around, mix your beautiful colors?" He was looking down, reading something she'd said word for word. "It's still therapy?" he read. "The only time you really forget your problems? Each painting or watercolor is like entering another world?"

Liddy stared at him.

To her surprise, Minton looked at her almost sadly. "I envy you," he said, smiling. "Very few people have that escape valve."

Nice to say, but that's *it*? His comment was kind but something any pal could have said – and they'd just spent fifty whole precious minutes accomplishing nothing. Liddy felt more than annoyed - then realized that annoyed is good; annoyed is wonderful; it banishes anxiety for a few minutes.

She rose, thanked, gave a polite good-bye more stiffly than she had on previous occasions, then stopped for a moment with her hand on the doorknob.

"One insight?" she said. He'd gotten up to see her out. "Someone suggested that the visions in the shower stall and on the loft glass and my dreams all *involve water*. She asked if I did water

74

sports, and I told her yes, a lot of my life has been swimming and boating."

Minton looked almost hurt. "Oh gosh, you've been seeing another psychiatrist."

No, a cop who's better than you, Liddy thought, stifling the urge to snark; reassuring him instead.

She actually walked the ten blocks home, realizing that shrinks were as lost as anyone else, you had to struggle yourself out of your own pits. The leg felt okay, and what surprised Liddy more was the fact that she felt okay - not great...but several notches better, and that was something to celebrate, wasn't it? The sun was warm, had dropped to its five-thirty softness coloring everything old-fashioned amber. Central Park West looked bathed in amber; ditto the passersby enjoying being out and the traffic moving slowly at its late Friday pace and the dog walkers getting pulled behind their happy, yipping charges. Squint: a nostalgic old postcard. Oh, it did feel good to be out. Nightmares and such were forgotten.

At Eighty-Sixth Street, standing on the corner, Liddy saw a FedEx truck pull up to the light. For a second Sasha Perry's face appeared on the truck's sun-glowing windshield, but the traffic light changed, the truck moved, and Sasha was gone.

For an instant *but why would the red teddy bear be wet?* came back to her, but she pushed it down; wanted to stay feeling good.

Imagination anyway, Liddy thought, walking on. That's all it is. Has to be...

19.

August was the worst, the absolute worst for trying to find anybody in Manhattan. Too many of them were just someplace else or off to the country or the shore – those who could afford it – and in the case of Ben Allen, he was half out the door and looked annoyed.

"You're late and I'm late for the ferry. Can we do this another time?"

Kerri apologized, the traffic was terrible. "Would you have preferred I use my siren?" she asked sweetly. "I could have been here in minutes with my siren blaring."

No, that wouldn't have looked good, a police officer screeching to the curb of the pretty West Village brownstone where this doctor had his office. She'd gotten him at a good time, too. Peering past him into his first floor doorway, she saw that his reception room and long reception counter were empty. Assistants and nurses had left for their weekends. Good.

A bit more finagling – she'd be quick, just a wee follow up - got him back into his inner office and looking tense behind his desk. He was tall, early forties with darting pale eyes, dark hair, and long fingers suddenly busy in his cell phone. He'd been interviewed before by the police, this doctor who'd made out Sasha Perry's uppers prescription which she'd written over, changed the dose. That had been uncomfortable for him, especially since other students had done the same. Was it his fault if they altered his prescriptions – or that one of the kids *said* he was the go-to doc for that? Prove he knew what they did! Harassment to put him on some damned watch list!

The police had been unable to prove anything, of course. And Kerri had never actually seen him since others had done his interview. Ah, but she had seen his picture in the cop logs; it just hadn't registered. It had taken a surprise six hours of sleep and then waking and re-thinking last night's researching...

...and it hit.

He was the third man in that Facebook picture with Paul Barron and Carl Finn before Barron's boat.

Now Kerri sat, simultaneously taking in the room with its diplomas and photos and re-thinking what she wanted to ask him – what suddenly needed updating.

"Sasha Perry," she said, leaning forward.

He nodded as if he'd expected the question, looked up from his cell phone, looked away. "I saw you on the news," he told a potted plant in the corner. "Awful business. Poor kid."

"Recent disclosures suggest that Sasha continued getting Adderall or generic amphetamines from a new source after she left you." It wasn't a complete lie: Becca Milstein suspected it, it sounded likely, and Kerri wanted to see this doctor's reaction. "Would you know anything about that?"

"No." His hand gestured as if pushing away the question. "And even if I did, patient privilege extends after a patient's demise – *if* that's what happened. I wouldn't divulge anything even if I knew – how would you imagine otherwise?"

Kerri said nothing, letting him squirm in the silence. She had researched him before coming. He disliked cops but was loved by poor people and students – treated many free of charge or took Medicaid as well as regular payment; also taught at the U and lectured tirelessly about HIV avoidance and the urgency of free college education. His big ego enjoyed his saintly status, his planned photo ops in old shirts and jeans at soup kitchens and free clinics and basketball with poor kids.

"You done?" asked the saint, fiddling with his cell phone,

muttering about Friday night ferry schedules to Fire Island.

"Well, I'm afraid your name's back on our minds," Kerri lied again. "We've had another arrest for falsifying narcotics prescriptions, this time tracing to a source *citing you as the referral*. What say you to that?"

He looked at her, then tried to laugh but paled a little. "Are you kidding?" He gestured angrily. "I wouldn't go near something like that. I had nothing to do with Ms. Perry's falsifying her prescription in the first place – now you're suggesting I'm involved in some kind of-"

"Network?" Kerri supplied, flicking another look around the room.

He leaned back, feigning disgust at this dumb cop's questions. "This is a silly conversation," he said, then got up. "Now if you'll excuse me."

Kerri stayed in her seat. "You live in Chelsea, don't you? On West 23rd in a penthouse with lovely gardens? And a gardener who comes in, and a basketball court at one end of the garden where you entertain friends and students and even hold an occasional fundraiser? I read about it."

"So?" His face stiffened.

"Those are expensive digs. Three million you paid for it two years ago?"

"What of it?"

"You treat many patients for free or just take Medicaid. Even with regular insurance, a garden penthouse in Chelsea is expensive for a physician, whereas illegal prescription drugs are big business, just *huge-*"

"I have inherited money. Goddammit, this is offensive."

Kerri looked at his left hand. "Not *that* much inherited, I checked." No, she hadn't; she had no idea how much he had and was winging this. She put her hand to her heart. "Really doctor, considering your fine work and the community adoration you've built, I'd hate to see your name back in the papers."

"Get out." His voice dropped and he glared. "I've given enough time to your bullshit."

Kerri rose. "Fine, it's your choice if you want to...obstruct." She emphasized the word, really dragged it out. "By the way - are you divorced yet or just separated?"

He froze.

She indicated his left hand. "Recently separated, I'm guessing. Ring tan line's still discernible. Did your wife insist that you wear it? Was that a bummer? I read about the domestic abuse calls to your home. I'd hate to see that too back in the news."

Allen stared at her; breathed in, swallowed. "I know why you're doing this."

Kerri stepped away from him, not answering. She had him defensive and limp now, not objecting to her survey of photos on the wall, more photos behind his desk.

"What's this?"

Allen barely glanced. "Photo of me with a homeless guy who needed meds. You're doing this because you're the one cop left vowed publicly to solve what happened to Sasha Perry. You want to *build your career* on that poor kid's-"

"Nonsense," she told him scornfully. "What's this?"

Barely glanced, seething. "It's a boat."

"Yours?" She'd seen it behind his desk the moment she entered.

"No! It's...faculty friends going out for a sail. Listen, it wasn't that *way* about my breakup. *She* was the abusive one, *she* was screwing around. It's harassment to threaten me with more media lies..."

He droned, so caught up in defending himself that he waved a tense hand - "Whatever!" - when she asked to take a quick picture of the grinning group before the docked sailboat. Ben Allen, Carl Finn and Paul Barron, with Finn planted boisterously in front of the other two, hamming it up and hoisting beer cases.

The same photo as on Carl Finn's Facebook page.

Her gut had led her here, now her heart pounded. She had felt her way through BS questions guessing that this doctor on Sasha's first faked prescription might have lead to...

Allen referred twice to Sasha as "that poor kid." She was troubled, he cared about her, knew the cops were watching him and may have sent her on to Carl Finn - also an M.D. but off authorities' radar.

Well, this was something: an established connection between the two men and Sasha.

Ben Allen was back in his chair, frowning and dour; barely responded when Kerri thanked him and left.

Why so troubled if he's clean? she wondered as she headed to her Bronco. Then stopped; felt her heart kick higher as she wondered how *much* Allen had cared about Sasha – then heard Becca again: *"Maybe it was some guy with a jealous wife or girlfriend."*

Huh? Wait a minute. She suddenly felt hyper.

The head was spinning. She needed someone to help her think, she decided, driving off.

20.

"Don't eat," she told Alex, peeling left, beating a yellow light.

"Ever?" he asked.

"No, now. Come to my place, I feel like cooking, have new thoughts about the Perry case and a raging need to get the hands busy instead of the busting head-" A horn blasted. She'd just swerved past an Audi on Eighth, had made it up to Midtown in record time.

"You speeding again?"

"Who me? Never!"

"You're going to get caught one of these days. Some rookie in blue's gonna pull you over and be really surprised."

"Won't happen."

"You also sound too energetic for Friday at six. That's not normal."

"I'm revved. Cooking helps me think - besides, how long since you've eaten healthy?"

"Not since you brought in that chicken Whatchamacallit."

"Marengo." It was an impulsive chance to slip in something else. "Doesn't your girlfriend cook?"

Hesitation, then: "Things aren't going so well there, she never cooked anyway. You just caught me going into that hoagie joint with its mystery meat and tomatoes that look like plasma."

"Don't eat in those places! E.coli! Salmonella! Come chez me!"

"I'm on my way."

He hung up with a whoop and Kerri calculated: he'd have to drive all the way up from his place in Chinatown, which gave her time. On 108th Street she stopped at her favorite market, picked up eats, and minutes later was unpacking at her home, a converted two bedroom way over on West 110th near Riverside Park with its jogging and picnic areas and dog walking trails if she had a dog, which she didn't, sigh.

She patted Gummy, her tabby who sidled over to rub her leg and then jump onto the counter. "Yes Gums, food, I'm happy to see you too," she said, scooping out tuna fish, putting the cat and her bowl back on the floor. "Whatsamatter, you bored with Kibbles 'n Bits?"

By the time she showered fast and was back to cutting and chopping, the bell rang, and there was Alex, one arm leaning on her jamb, the other holding up a pretty-wrapped bottle of wine.

"Shiraz your favorite," he smiled crookedly, coming in, pressing the bottle to her heart. He had showered and smelled of cologne and looked handsome – her soul swelled and she thought, cripes, maybe this wasn't such a good idea, especially with him checking her out like that in her form-fitting jeans and sleeveless blue cotton sweater and her hair flying not quite dry from her shampoo. He also seemed to anticipate awkwardness by marching straight to the center island, plunking the wine there, then stooping to greet Gummy. She purred; actually seemed to *smile* as he cooed and scratched behind her ears and then she jumped into his arms.

Holding her, he took one of the bar stools and watched Kerri, back to busy cutting, chopping, heating up a pan. He'd been here before, oh yes, and now looked happily around at her apartment's familiar openness, the warmth of bare brick that made up one wall, the sturdy beams of this old brownstone that dated back to the late 1800s.

"Let me help." He put Gummy down, hesitated for one last pat, then seemed to think of something else as he straightened and started to unwrap the wine. Just the ribbon he took off, though, then stepped behind Kerri, pulled to the nape of her neck her still-damp hair, and tied it with the ribbon. "There," he said. "Pretty."

Oh, the feeling of his fingers on her neck. Kerri flushed bad, feared it showed, smiled and mumbled something stupid about the mushrooms, the mushrooms, they had to be washed and sliced.

He turned back to the sink, splashed water, got to work on the mushrooms. "So tell," he said over the water. "What're these new thoughts about the Perry case?"

Over sizzling chicken breasts and onion slices she told him first about the visit to Ben Allen. He remembered the name. "Hostile. The cop investigating him…"

"Eddie Ruiz."

"Right. Eddie said he showed up with his lawyer first thing and started ranting about police brutality."

"That's him. *Very* big ego, has set himself up as the god of vulnerable people who worship him. So I went to see him, made up BS to get him to talk. Got those mushrooms ready?"

Alex did and turned with them, dumped them dripping into the hot skillet where they sizzled like fire crackers and made him grin. Chicken Stroganoff. They'd made this recipe together before.

"You've lost me," he said, watching her stir. "Why'd you go to Allen in the first place? Nothing stuck to him. Sasha faked his prescription, he claimed to know nothing and that was that."

"I went because A – I'd never seen him, talked to him, and B – there are new things I just found out." With tongs Kerri flipped a chicken breast, then another. "Mainly, when I saw that *he* taught at the U too…wait, I'm getting ahead of myself. It really starts with - remember I told you about that woman named Liddy who came in last night?"

"Partly. You passed me running to someplace."

"Now I'm catching you up." Kerri stirred the mushrooms and

onions, simultaneously telling about Liddy Barron, her night-mares and apparitions all involving water in some form. "Instead of looney tunes, that hit home because we'd just seen Sasha's photo of the Hudson she'd shared with Becca – and Liddy Barron's husband owns a boat, docks it at the 79th Street Boat Basin. He's a neuroscientist named Paul Barron. While research-ing him I found that his research partner is a dude named Carl Finn, *new* stop on the breadcrumb trail because - ta-dah! – Finn, Barron and Ben Allen all teach at the U, and they're pals. On Allen's wall there's a photo of them whooping it up in front of Barron's boat. I've got it in my cell phone, and the same pic's on Carl Finn's Facebook page. Think it's time to turn down the heat?"

"Yes. I'm confused but continue." Alex was laying out two places on the counter - knives, forks, napkins – as Kerri turned the heat lower, continued.

"Sorry if it's coming out in a jumble, that's where I need you to help me sort it out. So…from Ben Allen's photo – *which no cop would have noticed in June* - we now have a connection between him, Sasha, and Carl Finn, who is also, conveniently for Sasha, an M.D. A ladies man too, which she may have found out fast. You should see his Facebook photos hugging lots of women."

"A needy, pretty young thing. I'll bet he adored her on sight."

"What a thrill that would have been for her. A good-looking doc seeming to love and take care of her, she would have fallen madly for him, and trusted him…this is all guessing – my thoughts going wild."

"Let 'em, this is good."

"It gets better. Finn's in research not clinical practice, so off the radar aimed at regular docs re getting prescription drugs." Kerri stirred again; turned another chicken breast. "So that's my new theory: Allen sending Sasha on to Finn."

"Like a party favor."

84

"Funny you should say that, 'cause after I left Allen it occurred that he liked Sasha *a lot*. Actually emoted about her, hence, a wrinkle in my theory – such as a love triangle? Jealousy? On the other hand Sasha may have gotten too needy for Finn, demanding and in the way because he was simultaneously romancing some rich lawyer who may have gotten wind of his little toy and dumped him, suddenly disappeared from his Facebook page, so Sasha had to go. Isn't wildly confused wild guessing wonderful?"

"Yes. I gotta look up this Finn."

The heat was lowered. Kerri scooped in fat free sour cream and medium dry sherry and stirred it all. Alex groaned that it looked so good his brain just quit, he couldn't think on an empty stomach, so they opened the wine and sat and dug in, amid more groaning from Alex mimicking a porn movie over how good it was. "Healthy *and* luscious, oh God, oh God, I'm in heaven - make this often, bring it in to work?"

Kerri laughed and said yes.

But soon enough they got back to it, went through it all again, with Alex following the dots that Kerri had made. "So...Liddy Barron's water nightmares led to her husband who led to Carl Finn. Curious how things sometimes come together."

"Liddy came in because of yesterday's TV conference."

"Oh, right." He was in his phone checking out Carl Finn online, in his Facebook pictures, then switching back to photos Kerri had shown him of Finn and Liddy Baron's husband at their science gathering. Kerri had her phone out too, showing the photo of Allen, Barron, and Carl Finn before Barron's boat.

Alex pointed to Paul Barron. "He isn't an M.D.?"

"No, just Allen and Finn, though for sure Allen's been extra careful doling out prescriptions knowing he's being watched, and Sasha would have been wary of street dealers, online drugs. Who wouldn't be if you had a friendly doctor?"

Kerri watched Alex frown at Carl Finn in close up. "Liddy

Barron also claimed she sketched Sasha without ever having seen her. I saw the sketch, it was eerie - a match."

"How could she not know who it was?"

Kerri told him about Liddy's accident, her hospital stay coinciding with the news coverage of Sasha's disappearance, and someone telling her maybe she saw the girl's picture on the hospital TV, identified and remembered her sub-consciously.

"Got any room left?" she said. "I've got dessert."

They moved to the couch where she was scooping vanilla ice cream onto apple pie when her phone buzzed.

She checked the readout with surprise. "What's this?"

21.

There was one lamp on in the bedroom. She wanted it that way because that's how she felt: sad, full of dark shadows, lonely. This wasn't healthy, going through old stuff, trying to figure what to throw out, what to pack, but Paul was working and it was on her list. Finish sorting, finish filling those Bekins boxes. What stays? What goes? Surely not this beat-up old sweatshirt – ha – the one she'd wanted to get and couldn't that time Carl was trysting down in the berth and Paul didn't want to disturb him.

No, that stayed, went into this box on the right because it was a reminder of an angry day. A wearable symbol of the resentment she felt for Carl and the hold he always had over Paul. It was stupid and passive, really: when she wore the damned sweatshirt Paul had no idea it was her way of silent protest, weak and mute but somehow a comfort. What difference would it make anyway if she complained? She had tried; Paul had thrown up his hands as if she wasn't being fair; it had come to nothing. Funny how some old clothes can make you feel better.

Enough.

She started tossing things. Jeans really too far torn - out, into the box on the left. Ditto the ragged old Reeboks, the white T-shirt with the wine stain, the blue T-shirt with the VILLAGE DRUNK logo on it - why had she ever thought that was funny? The red T-shirt…

She stopped and stared at it. Blinked, held it up. In the shadowy end of the bed, it looked darker than she knew it was. She brought it to the head of the bed, sat again and touched its old fabric under the light. The stitching was frayed along the neckline, but the color was still as red as the day it was new. Red...red...she stared at it, remembering the red teddy bear of her dream. The *soaking* red teddy bear, swept away in the current with Sasha clinging to it.

Sasha. Her ear stud.

"Was I right about the teddy bear?" she had asked Kerri Blasco.

"Close. Very close," the detective had smiled and said.

Liddy's frustration returned over not being able to describe it. She had seen it and sketched it! Surely, somewhere in the recesses of her overburdened mind the stud was still there. She wanted to remember, really push to prove to herself that, despite everything, her mind still worked.

Small ball on top, bigger one below...kinda like a snowman. Right, stupid, a snowman in a red T-shirt.

Liddy raised her head; blinked. Something was coming. She stared at the closed curtain on the window as if it were a movie screen, and saw, focusing, not a snowman in a red T-shirt but... It focused further, and suddenly her heart took off because she had it, and jumped for her purse, found what she was looking for, then came back to the bed by the lamp and started punching her phone.

The other end picked right up. "Blasco."

"Winnie the Pooh!" Liddy cried. Then half-stammered identifying herself and said it again. "It just came to me. The ear stud of the blond girl who passed us that day was Winnie the Pooh."

"You're sure?" Kerri said cautiously.

"Yes, yes, I had one as a kid, have been seeing his little red T-shirt without realizing, obsessing about red in all sorts of crazy ways." Pause to gulp air. "I don't know if it helps, it's just nice to know I haven't totally lost my mind. I just...wanted to tell you."

"You nailed it," Kerri said quietly. Alex was by her on the couch. He'd been leaning on her but he straightened; got out his notebook.

Liddy sat hunched on the bed. Her surroundings had disappeared and her months of torment were now maybe explainable in the phone. "*Why* did I see her, can you tell me that? The news says no one else has, and out of the blue she comes to *me*? Why?"

"I wish I knew, Liddy. You did see her on television." It was a still-cautious, trick comment.

"Not close enough to see any ear stud which she wasn't wearing anyway! You said it wasn't in any photos released!"

She'd nailed it again. Kerri glanced at Alex as Liddy went on, "It's as if she's sought me out for some reason. Why me? Please...help me understand her?"

Tell her, Alex scrawled fast.

Kerri did, speaking quietly. She knew Sasha's story. Her heart pounded. This was something.

"The Winnie the Pooh ear stud was a gift from Sasha's father, when she was fourteen. Her mother had died years before, and she loved her dad terribly. She was from a small town upstate, got a scholarship to NYU – which thrilled them – but when she came here her dad came too, saying he wanted the best for her but couldn't bear being alone. He met a nice woman, married her, then died at the end of Sasha's junior year. She took it horribly. Her stepmother said she'd worn the ear stud occasionally before that. Afterwards, she wore it a lot."

Liddy listened, tears stinging. "So sad," was all she could manage. "Yes."

Liddy voice felt strangled. "But if I saw her, she must be alive."

Silence at the other end, and then: "But why would she give heartache to everyone who loved her? Her stepmother said she wouldn't do that in a million years."

"So did I see a ghost?" Liddy gripped her phone harder.

"I've got no answers. Except that your ID of the stud has me reeling. Who knows? Sometimes people have emotional breakdowns and just...lose it, go into hiding. Possibly Sasha *is* in your neighborhood for some reason. Thanks for calling, you're a sweet soul. Please definitely call if anything else."

Liddy hung up and sat, wiping her eyes with the red T-shirt. Incongruously, not thinking at all, she whimpered, "I'm from upstate too." Then she inhaled, closed her eyes and thought, That's it. I remembered and my part is done. Get packing. Climb out of this.

At Kerri's end, the ice cream and apple pie had turned to mush. They'd lost interest in it. Kerri stared at once-hot sugary goo congealing as Alex scribbled notes.

"Ear stud?" he asked.

She explained that part of Liddy's interview.

"Whoa," he said.

Kerri kept staring at the pie mush. "I don't know what to make of this." Their shoulders were touching. She picked up her phone; stared at its screen holding Sasha's picture of the Hudson. "Except…the feeling just got stronger that everything points to this, like a compass needle."

"So what next?" Alex was in his phone too, scrolling back, back, through Carl Finn's Facebook posts.

"I want to know more about him." Kerri tapped his phone. "Curious there's no pics of Sasha."

"She may have complained, which was her undoing. Or maybe – oh hell – maybe we've been making the wrong guess all along because..." Kerri gripped her brow as if it hurt. Alex put his arm around her.

"I'm back to thinking of Ben Allen," she said. "He recently broke up with his wife…infidelities abounding… Remember Becca saying she'd suspected maybe some guy with a jealous wife or girlfriend?"

On her phone Kerri showed Alex ShadowFace, enlarged from Becca's selfie. "That look like any of those men?"

"Finn, I think, but still…"

"I know. Circumstantial."

She leaned on his shoulder, closed her eyes. "My head hurts bad."

He drew her closer, kissed her brow. "You'll think of something," he said quietly. "In the meantime..." He inhaled. Didn't need to say the words, they had been in the air since he'd walked in the door.

But they came out anyway. "Can I stay?"

The question evoked memories of waking up anxious, leaving separately ("sneaking out," Kerri had called it), coming into the squad room as if nothing, avoiding each other's eyes so obviously that others *guessed*, then rumors spread and all hell broke loose. Cops were the worst gossips.

Kerri snickered as if something was funny. "No, you can't stay. I have a headache."

Alex rose, nodding. "We have to think." His arm went back around her. "Get serious sleep, tackle these things with clear minds."

At the door Kerri leaned into him, murmuring sorry about the headache.

He reached behind her neck, pulled free the ribbon he'd tied there, and put it to his lips. "Mm, smells sweet."

He kissed her again and left, holding the ribbon.

22.

Suddenly, things were moving fast – exciting, really – with swept-away red teddy bears and the crying young blonde pushed down under the tumult of movers coming and going and a dining room table that wouldn't fit in the padded freight elevator. By three o'clock on Monday, August 18th, Liddy and Paul's furniture was trucked to the loft. When the dust settled, Paul went to his lab while Beth and a workman helped Liddy set up her easel and draftsman table and art supplies in her new studio with its shelves and blue-upholstered window seat and bright birch floor – Charlie Bass's old floor had only needed a good polish. The alarm guy came too to wire the studio separately, so the top sash could open with the alarm still on to let out toxic turpentine fumes.

They spent Monday night at The Mercer, a hip hotel with loft-like rooms and a four poster bed. On Tuesday, August 19th, they moved in officially to their new home. Paul kissed Liddy and left two hours later for his lab while she spent the rest of the day unpacking sheets and towels and putting clothes in drawers and closets and then plates and glasses in the old Spanish armoire which looked wonderful in the kitchen.

Around six, a red-bowed Williams and Sonoma espresso machine with little cups arrived from Beth. Lab assistants sent a big plant – ha - just what the place needed; another friend Ben Allen sent a nautical-themed lamp; and Carl Finn sent a carton of California champagne with a note that said, *Here's to this celebration and amazing celebrations ahead. Cheers to you both on your great new adventure.*

Now Liddy was happy – thrilled, actually. She'd gone three

nights with good sleep and no nightmares. Paul had been practically euphoric their celebratory night at the Mercer – he'd ordered champagne; his love had been wild and driving – and that ebullient feeling carried over into the chore of settling in. On the next day Liddy found a supermarket on Wooster and a bakery on Spring Street; hung pots and pans over their cook top; sprayed the plants (no ghosts, oh joy), went out again and found a Victorian glass lamp for the living room. It wasn't heavy, wrapped in its package, so Liddy browsed more; stopped before Pete's Old Books, and gazed into the window. There, near the front, was a DVD of *Vampire Island*, the movie Charlie Bass had been in.

There was something loving about the way it was displayed. The movie hadn't had much success but there it was, in front with current and classic hits, a whole stack of them with one copy facing out. Had Charlie Bass frequented this store? Been a friend? Was this a tender monument to an actor who had lived just doors away?

Liddy went inside and bought a copy. The owner was out but a young assistant told her yes, Charlie used to come here, hang out. "He was always over there in the corner reading." The young man pointed to a battered chair. "Really a sweet guy. We miss him."

Liddy left with the DVD.

Still felt so ebullient that she bought two fat pastrami sandwiches wrapped in aluminum foil and walked – a bit painful but good exercise - the six blocks to Paul's lab; walked past grad students working at lines of microscope-studded counters to Paul and Carl's workstation. They had a long counter to themselves.

"Brought lunch," she smiled as Paul in his white coat looked up surprised from a mouse cage; then Carl feet away in his white coat turned from talking to a third man not in a white coat.

"Oh," Liddy said. "Hi Ben."

Ben Allen, Carl's friend more than Paul's, gave her a quick smile. "Hey, Liddy, congrats! You're all moved in, I hear."

She thanked him for the lamp; he gave another easy smile that somehow went with his usual outfit: a blazer over an old polo shirt with jeans and scruffy cross trainers, which she saw as he rushed from behind the counter to greet her. When was the last time she'd seen him? May? No – she had a dim memory of him coming to the hospital. With his floppy dark hair he looked younger than forty-two. There was something else about him she was trying to remember…

"I brought sandwiches," she told him awkwardly, putting them and the lamp package on the counter. Also awkward was seeing Paul and Carl turned away from her, muttering tensely. "Just two," she told Ben, touching her bulging deli bag. "Sorry, I didn't know you were here."

He waved a hand as if nothing. "Just heard Paul's selling his boat. Came to say I'm in pain – I won't be able to borrow it anymore."

"Buy your own?" she suggested - and he laughed easily. "Funny you should mention it, the thought crossed my mind." He turned. "Just what I need, right Carl? More headaches, upkeep and expense?"

Carl gave a tense smile, went back to his discussion with Paul. They seemed to be arguing about a white mouse in a small cage with a blue stripe on its fur. The blue stripe meant it had survived its first experiment. Other mice scratched around in cages stacked further down the counter, some with red stripes, meaning they had survived more than one test and were up for more. Mice with purple stripes were sprawled in their cages still alive but not for long. Their brains would wind up in cross sections on the researchers' office monitors.

Liddy hated what they did and suddenly regretted having come. Neither Paul nor Carl had mentioned the sandwiches. She felt as if she were intruding.

But Ben saved the moment.

"Hey," he said, chucking her arm. "That video you took of us doing the Long Island Regatta? You were going to send it to me." Then he caught himself; looked contrite. "Oh sorry, your memory..."

Liddy assured him with her own apology. She was getting better and should have remembered. "Here, I'll send it to you now."

Out came their two cell phones, and she sent him the video. "Awesome, thanks," he said; then turned again to Paul, Carl, and their mice.

"Hey, you geeks, want to take a break? See some sailing?"

Liddy grabbed the sandwiches, and minutes later the four of them were in Paul and Carl's shared office behind the counter: two desks, screens, monitors showing dissected rodent brains, stacks of papers, science journals, and more mouse cages. The room smelled of mice and antiseptic.

Paul thanked Liddy for the sandwiches, looked at his inside its foil, put it on his desk. Carl gave a brusque, "Yeah, thanks," and bit into his as Ben Allen hooked his phone up to one of the monitors and turned the light down.

Next, male hoots and hollering as waves splashed and wind blew and the three of them grinned and struggled with the rigging and bringing her about. "We're gaining, do *not* lose this!" Carl Finn yelled in the video; and Ben, standing next to Liddy, said, "Guess you're done with regattas, huh?"

"Definitely," she said. "Second time I got seasick and skinned knees. Just give me a rowboat on a smooth lake."

Then she thought, funny how I remembered that day. It just...came. On the monitor the boat listed wildly, came dizzyingly close to tipping, and for a moment she even felt seasick; put her hand on a counter to steady herself. It came back to her too that Ben had been thrilled at the near capsize. "Adrenalin, adrenalin!" he'd shouted. In a flash Liddy remembered him getting splashed with freezing water and loving it. She wracked her brain for something else that nagged about him. No dice.

Carl and Paul were engrossed in the video. In the dimness Liddy felt suddenly alone in all this maleness…but there was something else. Some tension she felt between Paul and Carl, just watching them, their body language.

She tugged at the elbow of Paul's white coat and said, "I should go."

"Okay," he said, unresponsive, looking neither at her nor the video.

She left feeling troubled; hurt, actually. Almost forgot the lamp package she'd left on their counter, ran back for it, and heard Carl again.

"Do *not* lose this!"

23.

Sketching helped banish hurt, so back in her studio she googled Charlie, found a photo of him she liked, and lost herself in his sad features. Minutes later his dark, mournful eyes stared out at her from her sketch. She stared at it for long moments; felt him there with her, with the shelves and cozy-for-reading window seat he had created. He'd been a kindred spirit, she realized, and wished she had known him.

Paul was home by eight, but touchy and fretful that their deadline was looming. He barely noticed the bouillabaisse Liddy had made, but she soothed, reminded him of his favorite line from their poor days: "Without deadlines, nothing would get done."

"That was before the big time," Paul groused, poking at a shrimp. "Carl was on me today about the time lost to the move."

His euphoria lasted for two days? Now that the move was *done* he'd gone immediately back to tension? "Don't let Carl dictate how you feel," Liddy urged. "You're just as brilliant."

He left the table muttering about doing more work at home. Liddy sighed and straightened up as Paul went to the living room with his computer. Then in her studio she rolled out new canvas, slit it with her box cutter, cut it neater with her long sharp scissors, then stapled it onto wooden stretchers. *Bang! Bang!* went her staple gun, the sound making her feel better, telling her that she was really back on track with her painting. Final move-in things could wait, be done gradually. Tomorrow or the next day she'd finish her Rawlie-the-space-warrior painting and the woman-running-in-rain watercolor, then start new projects that were overdue; two publishers had emailed to complain.

While priming a canvas she stopped, frowning a little, and turned to face the living room.

It had been awfully quiet out there. Usually, if Paul worked at home, he'd be sporadically on his phone with Carl or one of their assistants comparing lab notes they'd made during the day, discussing chemical structures, modification compounds, anesthetic activity on tadpoles then - oh good, move the new one up to mice.

There'd been nothing. No sound that she had heard.

Because she'd been so preoccupied?

She went out to look.

Saw Paul standing at the dimmed window, slightly bent with his back to her, peering through the telescope.

"Hey," she said quietly, almost tentatively though she wasn't sure why. He said "hey back" but didn't straighten. She crossed the living room with one lamp lit, stood next to him and looked down. Below, the street was a dazzling nightlife stage, busy with partiers, traffic, happy drunks running from bars and restaurants to dance and live music clubs. The sound was muted by the double-pane glass.

"Takin' a break from work?" she asked in the same hesitant tone.

"Yup."

"Get much work done?"

"Half. I'm tired. So damn tired."

She noticed that the angle of his 'scope was aimed higher than the street; tilted up to what had to be windows across the way.

"Looks fun. Can I have a peek?"

"Sure," he said a bit tightly, tilting the telescope back down to the street before he stepped aside for her.

Why did he do that?

She looked in, adjusted the eyepiece, swept the 'scope over the street scene. Then she raised the barrel to the angle he'd had it at, and found herself looking into someone's bedroom. The bed was wildly rumpled, empty for a moment and then it wasn't, with a naked man and woman climbing back into it and somehow still managing to keep the sex going. He was holding her up by the buttocks, pounding away as he threw her back onto the bed and fell on top of her. Wow, look at him go. He must be on speed or something...

Enough. Liddy looked back to Paul and attempted levity.

"What do you bet they fell out of bed."

"Who?"

"That couple having wild crazy sex."

"I didn't see anyone having sex." He was back on the couch, his tone announcing that he was concentrating, couldn't be disturbed. He shifted; scowled harder into his computer.

Liddy stood, uncertain, bursting to say something profound or funny like the old answered prayers thing: you get what you've been wanting - and it comes with side effects. Soho was full of distractions for nose-to-the-grindstone types like them. But still, Liddy thought again, Paul had gotten his wish! They were all moved, back on track, and she was sleeping well and feeling happy – pretty much, though she hadn't been too sure of that since her visit to the lab.

She exhaled and let him work. Returned to her studio where she re-capped her primer and put her staple gun and box cutter on a high shelf, her long sharp scissors on her draftsman table. Then she washed up, called a soft good-night to barely a grunt back, and went to bed.

24.

She felt bad. Was trying to sleep when Paul came to bed too.

"You awake?" he whispered after a minute.

"Yes."

He exhaled hard. "Sorry I was in a foul mood tonight."

"I understand."

"I should be totally happy – and I am except for..."

"I know, the research."

He was silent, just a dark profile on the pillow next to her. Then he said, "It's not that."

She turned her head to him.

In the dimness she saw him take a breath. "Something else," he said, and swallowed. "Carl was seriously grim this morning, worse than usual. Finally he told me." Another deep breath. "Before I got there the police came to visit him, asking questions about that missing coed. They'd been to question Ben, too, but seem more focused on Carl."

Liddy stared at him.

"It was a female detective." Paul's voice speeded up. "That night at Chez Pierre you said you'd gone to tell the cops you'd maybe seen that girl. You mentioned the detective you talked to and said, *'she was nice'* so it must have been the same one."

Liddy almost laughed. "There are many female detectives, why assume-"

"I've assumed, okay? It's too much of a coincidence, and Carl said he recognized her. They were showing her on the news, she's the last and only cop left investigating that case –now bothering Carl and it couldn't come at a worse time."

"This is crazy." A tremor crept into Liddy's voice. "What…are they asking him?"

"*She*. Her last name is Blasco. Sound familiar?"

No reply, but the heart was thudding. "What possible connection…what did she…"

"Got nowhere. Asked Carl if he'd known that missing girl Sasha and he said no; said she acted pleasant enough, but he couldn't figure why the hell she came to question him. Then he asked me if *you* had anything to do with it. Of course I said no - but Lids, this isn't good. We can't *have* this."

It took a second; then it hurt. "Who's '*we?*' You and Carl, or you and me?"

"Us too." Paul's voice rose. "Hell, the research is our *future*."

The heart throbbed, but she frowned. "Why would Carl connect me with this?"

"He remembered your sketch, had seen that girl's picture in the news."

"That's ridiculous! Sasha Perry's been all over the news!"

"Right, but why would a cop be coming after *him*?"

This was an ambush. Liddy tried to control her breathing and Paul went grimly silent. A long, bitter moment passed; then: "Have you ever realized," she said tremulously, "that we know nothing about Carl? What he does in his off hours – God, his women alone, he's like a *collector*, and his violent breakup with his wife? 'Cassie wouldn't tolerate my long hours,'" she mimicked. "That's a lie! He screwed around and was rotten to her and *knows we know and keeps repeating that lie.* Is he delusional or just a pathological liar?"

"Neither, he's just…" Paul seemed to run out of steam; waited another minute, then rolled to Liddy on the pillow. "He's just Carl. He's always been like that. The cop visit set him off on me; that's what was really bugging and I'm sorry."

Liddy lay stiffly, saying nothing. Paul put his hand over hers.

"Anyway it's over," he said. "She came, asked her questions, got nothing and left." He patted Liddy's hand. "I'd promised myself I wouldn't even bring it up, but I did and I'm kicking myself. We friends again?"

"Friends," she said dully.

"Your hand is cold."

No answer.

"Try to sleep."

"Okay."

"We'll both feel better in the morning."

"Right. Paul?"

"Um?"

"Why did Ben come to the lab today?"

She felt him exhale in the darkness. "Carl called him after the police visit."

"That's funny. He told me he'd just heard about you selling the boat, was in pain about it."

"Ridiculous. He's known for a week."

"He's as phony as Carl." And then, like a wild flash, it came back, something Liddy had heard - when? In the hospital? Some news report?

"I...remember now. Sasha was arrested for falsifying a narcotics prescription...written by Ben."

"Yeah, I heard them arguing about that - part of it anyway, I wasn't included. Ben's still humiliated he was dragged into that. Maybe they're bothering him again since this thing has resurfaced."

"But why would Carl call him after this morning?"

"Who knows?" Paul's voice was fading. "To commiserate? That Blasco's probably bothering a lot of people. Leave it, Lids, please? I'm blitzed, can we please go to sleep?"

He rolled back to his pillow. Minutes passed, his breathing got heavier, then he slept.

Liddy lay, thinking about Kerri Blasco and the resulting uproar at the lab. Should she feel guilty? No, dammit, she'd done what she felt morally pulled to do - which raised the next question: *Why* did Kerri want to question Carl? What did she suspect that led her to him?

Then came a question that nagged even more: could all the horrid nightmares, fears and hallucinations be really closer to her than Liddy imagined? Was *that* why Sasha's sketch just jumped from her hand that first Sunday in Soho?

Things came together.

She tried not to feel angry at Paul.

Leave it, Lids, please?

As in, don't rock the boat – is that what he was really saying? Had he planned that whole bedtime conversation?

He'd hurt her earlier, she'd gone to bed feeling bad, then he'd timed his coming to bed full of "what really bothered" him: Stay out of it, Lids, don't even go near the cops, Lids, Carl must not be disturbed, the research, the research.

Because Paul's scientific takeoff was on the line, too.

Liddy blinked into the darkness, letting that last thought sink in. It took hold and wouldn't let go. She remembered – waking last Friday morning - her nightmare of drowning and Paul swimming away from her, saving himself. A terrible dream! For four days she'd pushed it down and now it was back, she was seeing again the bubbles coming from her nose, the blue circle of sky above getting smaller, the boat's hull on the surface and Paul's legs kicking, swimming back up as the blond girl touched her shoulder, took the teddy bear and was swept away crying. The dream had her trembling with her chest heaving again. She had seen it and felt it all over again.

The clock read three. What? Had she drifted off? Slept and redreamt it? She must have, because seconds ago the clock just read one.

This was bad. She needed to sleep. Wanted to paint tomorrow, catch up and do good work...

Distraction, maybe a distraction would help.

Read a little? Turn the TV on low?

She crept out of bed and went back to the telescope.

25.

Someone down in the street was throwing up. A girl yards away in a sequined dress was yelling at a cab that passed her. Couples were moving but more slowly, weaving. A man danced alone, seemed to be trying to imitate the graceful arm sweeps and pirouettes of *Swan Lake*.

Charlie Bass considered this telescope better than cable TV, Beth said. It was. Not for anything prurient, it was just an amazing, fascinating eye into the real human condition, after the makeup smears and the booze turns the belly sour and the whole masquerade is over...kind of like Poe's *Masque of the Red Death*, Liddy thought, only nobody was dying down there, not of plague or anything else from what she could see. Just drunks trying to get home and cabs refusing to stop for them. Every New Yorker's idea of desperation.

This was good. It was taking her mind off herself and her obsessing. Liddy raised the telescope barrel to apartment windows across from her.

And up in the wild sex couple's bedroom...

...they were arguing.

No, they were dressed and fighting. Through their window a soundless scream fest of hunched accusations and jutting jaws and then...Liddy's lips parted...he hit her. Slammed her hard so she spun around crying - and then Liddy saw her face.

Couldn't be.

She was young. Her blond hair whipped her features as she wheeled and fell to the floor, out of sight. There'd been only that split second, but Liddy drew back from the telescope, stunned.

Close - but Sasha Perry? Couldn't be, just the mind playing tricks at something terrible. A man hitting a woman. Liddy felt sick.

In a jerky movement she twisted the eyepiece, feeling her heart throb as she peered through again. The bedroom was empty. Had the girl run out with the man in pursuit? Liddy tilted the barrel down. They weren't in the street. A different arguing couple was further down near the corner.

She panned the bedroom again. He'd been only half dressed - shirtless, dark pants looking yanked on, while the girl had gotten back into some kind of black party dress with its bodice torn. A dark, empty bottle lay near a strewn pillow.

Still no sign of them on the street. Maybe they'd gone into another room to simmer down? Continue the fight in winding down glowers and recriminations?

No telling, but what Liddy had seen shook her - on top of the fact that the girl for that split second had looked like Sasha Perry.

She couldn't be sure. Far from it.

Sometimes people have emotional breakdowns and just lose it, go into hiding, Kerri Blasco said. *Possibly Sasha* is *in your neighborhood for some reason. Please definitely call if anything else.*

But this wasn't something else – couldn't be – just an awful sighting witnessed by an overwrought mind that was seeing double from fatigue, not thinking right, and starting to doubt herself. Crazy, what the three a.m. of the soul can do to you. Because rising too was a new feeling of guilt toward Paul, and those paranoid thoughts she'd had about him. He'd worked so hard all his life; knocked himself out to give her happiness and this new start. Why had she even had that awful dream? Fear, that's all. Admit it, scared little weenie: fear of losing him, upsetting him, losing their relationship.

The abused blonde – Liddy's mind rushed back to her as she took one last look through the 'scope. No sign of her, and she hadn't come out of the building. So…maybe crying or simmering down or sleeping it off in another room and he's on the couch? There was no way to know. Liddy still made a mental note of which building, which floor, which window.

Then, shuddering, still seeing that girl get cruelly slammed, she went back to bed. Lay and struggled with the image, with her whole flashing storm of questions including…again wondering furiously why Kerri wanted to question Carl.

Something Alex Minton said came back to her: *The psyche seizes on a 'diversion cause' - something that's easier to deal with than the real issue. Some repressed memories are so terrifying that one is unable to remember, let alone face.*

Is that what I'm doing? Liddy fretted. Seizing on mistreated young women to divert me from something in my own life?

She dismissed the thought. That abused, crying girl did look like Sasha Perry, she did, she did…

Outside, a high siren wailed. Other street sounds came dimly through the window.

Strung tight as piano wire, Liddy stared into the deepest shadows of the room, knowing it might be hours before she could sleep.

26.

"He's the guy."

"You can't be sure."

"I haven't finished, don't stop me, I'm on a roll."

It was five minutes to eight. Kerri, in a blouse and gray pant suit today, was in the coffee-smelling break room with Buck Dillon and Jo Babiak, telling about her visit yesterday to Carl Finn, talking fast because they had a conference meeting at 8:15 with Lieutenant Tom Mackey presiding. She'd already filled them in on everything, as she had with Alex, from Liddy Barron's visit and interview, to Liddy's husband's M.D. pals, and Sasha's photo of the Hudson. She'd also told how Liddy had finally remembered Sasha's Winnie the Pooh ear stud, which had never appeared in any released photo. Sipping decaf with one hand, Kerri used her other hand to jab Carl Finn's face in her open laptop. It was the Facebook shot of him embracing the hard-looking corporate lawyer blonde who'd dumped him around the time of Sasha's disappearance.

"I called first, asked when he'd be in, and somebody who'd been working all night said he usually came in around eight. So I went before that; was just sitting there in his office when he walked in - ha, ambush! Didn't look at all happy when I introduced myself. Looked even unhappier when I said I was looking into Sasha's disappearance."

Buck, finishing an Egg McMuffin and eyeing a box of granolas, asked, "How long were you there?"

"A whole nine minutes before he threw me out. It was enough, I got him shook, took mental notes – and there's more." Kerri took the granola box from Buck, glanced in, looked back to the other two. "Of course he said he didn't know Sasha, never laid eyes on her, blah blah, the usual. But, I asked, wasn't she part of the University and taking the human biology courses that he taught? No, must've been somebody else's human biology course, it was a big department, he'd never laid eyes on the girl."

Kerri looked back into the granolas, chose one with chocolate chips, started peeling off the wrapper.

"Tons of sugar *and* healthy," Jo Babiak muttered, scrolling through Carl Finn's Facebook pictures. She was thin and worked out every day.

"Yeah, that's what the label says. Gee, you mean they lie?" Kerri took a good chomp, checked her watch because they had to jet, and tried to talk with her mouth full.

"He's not smart, knows nothing about avoiding deceptive behavior. *Perps* are better at it than this guy. He flees eye contact, hesitates and processes every answer – I even asked him who cleaned the mouse cages to get a base line reaction – he looked away before answering even *that*. Had his chair pushed way back from his desk so he could cross his legs and swivel his chair and look anywhere but at me. Was sweating, too. Developing a nice sheen on his brow and upper lip – kept wiping his mouth and pulling at his lower lip."

"The most common tell," Buck said, getting up, going to the counter for more coffee.

"He's a classic narcissist, too," Kerri said. "Kept telling me how important his time was to humanity that I was taking. Started saying that after I'd been there for just six minutes."

"So?" Buck came back and sat with his filled mug. "You've established that he's a jerk and then he kicked you out. This is the great discovery you wanted to tell us?"

"Nope."

And here Kerri grinned. Sat back in her chair, threw her

hands up, got philosophical but still spoke fast. "Y'know how in every investigation, it's often the serendipities that give the biggest boost? So there I was, kicked out after threats to holler police harassment and call his lawyer, and I'm walking down the aisle past lines of counters by now filling up with students in white coats and hospital scrubs running in with instrument trays – a long, very uptight room - and I passed the last counter up front, saw a heavyset girl in spectacles searching frantically through her box of slides…and right in front of her, honest to God, propped up against something, I saw a Winnie the Pooh, a big tubby one in his red T-shirt, like for a little girl."

The other two detectives looked at her. Jo Babiak was suddenly alert. "Winnie," she said.

"Yup. So I stopped and asked her about it, went all 'Oh isn't that adorable, so cute, it brings back my childhood - is that from your childhood too?'"

They were looking at her, barely blinking. "Tell," Buck said. "The suspense is killing me."

Kerri gave a smug face, leaned forward again. "The girl – her name tag said Sue Riley - said, 'No, *Carl gave it to me.*' He told Sue a little girl had given it to him, and it was sweet but he didn't think Winnie looked quite right in his office."

"A little girl gave him the Winnie the Pooh…" Jo said, clearly thinking about that wording. "Theoretically, circumstantial at best, he could have considered Sasha a little girl. A needy and annoying little girl."

"After the sweet young thing part wore off." Buck frowned thoughtfully at the tabletop. "Old story, huh?"

"This gets better," Kerri said. "I got all impressed, went Oh, wasn't that nice of him – then asked Sue *when* Finn gave it to her." Kerri raised her brows. *"Early last May.* She'd been worried about her exams and gone in to talk to him. He told her she was doing okay, then with his huge munificence gave her Winnie saying the

110

little girl had just given it to him. Sue said she almost fainted. 'Carl's so handsome, so brilliant, he did such a nice thing for me,' she said - actually blushed as she said it."

"Christ, early May?" Jo gaped at Kerri.

"Pinpointed exactly," Kerri said. "I told her oh gee, I had so much stress too - could I take a picture to help cheer me? And she said sure, take all you want, it's really a comfort, having Winnie sitting there right by me. So I took pictures. Close ups, plus mid distance of her whole work station in the U's lab." Kerri held her phone up. "Got 'em here, including one of her holding Winnie. Her name's right on her plastic name tag."

"So she can be subpoenaed," Jo mused, checking her watch, glancing over as someone else ran in for a quick Styrofoam cup of coffee. "It's something, but still circumstantial."

"But a *big* breadcrumb on the trail," Kerri countered. "Carl Finn knew Sasha, I *feel* it, he gave it away. His most deceptive behavior was when I asked about her being in his human biology class – which ran into a road block because next I called the U's administration clerk, who said there's no record of Sasha taking his class. That has to be wrong – he was sweating bullets over that. I asked him twice, he squirmed worse the second time."

"Dead end there." From Buck, with a headshake.

"Maybe," Kerri said, "But this guy's a focus like I haven't before felt. *Ever.*"

They got up, started clearing their cups and wrappers.

"Devil's advocate," Jo said, exhaling with the mix of frustration and excitement that Kerri clearly felt. "What if you find he knew her, even dated her? You've still got a whole lot of circumstantial."

"No. If it turns out he knew her at all, that's obstruction. I'd have him for that, at least. Take it from there. Keep digging."

111

27.

At eight she woke with a jolt, trembling, remembering the battered girl and the drowning dream. Paul was sitting by her on the bed. He'd brought her coffee and toast, and made a pained sound when she said she'd had a bad night.

"How much did you sleep?"

"Maybe four hours."

He grimaced. "I feel awful. I got you upset."

Something déjà vu about this morning's apology. He was dressed and showered; had cut his cheek shaving; touched where he'd put a dab of tissue to the place and shook his head. "Just when you'd started to sleep well again."

"Tonight will be better," she sighed.

The apartment smelled of burnt toast. She reached to his cheek where his tissue dab was bleeding through. "Ouch," she said.

"Yeah, I've gotta change it." He went back to the bathroom. Liddy pulled on her blue kimono and went to the kitchen. The toaster was unplugged and pulled out from the wall. Two slices of burnt toast lay strewn on the counter next to it; also a fork, just left there. Liddy peered into the toaster's dark recess. Subsequent bread slices had clearly toasted okay, but why did Paul leave the burnt ones just sitting there? Even rushing, that wasn't like him.

In a minute he was in the kitchen with a new tissue dab on his cheek, pacing, checking his texts and voice mails, starting to text back.

"Wait," Liddy said.

He looked at her.

She sank to one of the barstools; gestured feebly. "Last night-"

"I said I was sorry."

"Right, this is something else."

His look changed to, *oh Lids, what now?*

But she plunged, described fast and nervously what she'd seen. "Three in the morning. He hit her hard. It was awful."

"Terrible," he said, scowling back to a text.

"Shouldn't we do something?"

His phone dinged with another call. He raised it to read and shook his head, though whether in reaction to the call or to what Liddy had described, she couldn't tell.

"People argue, Lids. People fight. It's not our business."

He headed out of the kitchen, going on about the pitfalls of looking into people's bedrooms at three in the morning. "They're either asleep or having their worst moments."

"Wait, there's more." She followed him through the living room to the door, where he was grabbing his keys and laptop from a side table.

"For a second," she blurted, "I thought that girl might be her."

"Who?"

"Sasha Perry." She sounded ridiculous to herself, but out it burst. "At three I was tired, doubting myself, but now I've got this strong feeling it *was* her. She's holed up across the street with some guy who's abusing her."

Paul stopped what he was doing. Grimly, he put his things back on the table, reached out and held Liddy's shoulders. "Oh honey," he said, much too gently. He pulled her closer and inhaled; said slowly, almost sorrowfully, "Remember, in the old apartment, you thought you saw a couple fighting across the way? I looked out and there was no one there. Just shades pulled down to noisy air conditioners." He reached one of his hands to smooth her hair back. His fingers were cold.

"But..." she said with her face working.

"That new couple you saw, they've probably already made up or broken up and gone their separate ways. It happens all the time." He paused uncomfortably. "As far as all young blondes looking alike…"

Liddy turned away from him, feeling torn.

"Lids." He pulled her back to him, pulled her so close with his arms tight around her that she could feel his heart banging through their chest walls.

"Are you gonna be okay?" His tone was almost begging. "These…things – they're all connected to your…getting better. Please, tell me you're going to have a good day – oh God, the bad sleep."

"No, I'm okay."

He brightened. "Rapture. So tell me you'll have a good day, and paint beautiful paintings, and look smiling and pretty for tonight."

"Tonight?" Liddy was confused.

"Dinner out with Carl. I told you - when? Sunday? He just texted, cops all forgotten, reminding he wants to have dinner with us, help us celebrate the move."

The shoulders slumped and she nodded. *Oh hell…Carl.*

"I forgot," she said.

"I probably said it in a mad rush, we've both been under pressure." Paul turned to pick up his things. "I almost forgot too."

Liddy watched him, telling herself that by the light of day with the sun streaming through the windows, what he said about that fighting couple could be right – they'd either made up or called it quits. Fights happened all the time.

She took a deep breath. "Now I remember what you said about Carl word for word. Dear o.c. hard-working-except-for-women Carl wants to take a whole two hours off to celebrate at Righetti's, then you're both going back to the lab." She squared her shoulders. "Right, got it." She managed a smile.

Paul looked more relieved; looked suddenly expansive, in fact.

"There's another reason tonight's going to be special. A surprise."

"Surprise?"

"Yup." He grinned. "I've been trying not to even hint, but – see? I'm lousy at keeping secrets. So you're up for tonight?"

"I'll be ready, gorgeous and smiling. What's the surprise?"

"Not telling, and you left out relaxed. Please forget what I said about Carl last night. He was just upset."

"Sure." *Not likely*.

"Will you meet us at the restaurant? We're going straight there from work."

Liddy said yes. Paul gave her a hurried hug, and left.

And the bad, nagging feeling came back.

Conflict: obsess about that battered young woman and Sasha Perry (assuming they weren't one and the same), versus pushing it down, avoiding more stress in their lives.

The conflict grew in the shower, where at least there were no weeping faces on the wall.

In the bedroom Liddy dressed in jeans and a T-shirt; then, slowly, sat down by her pillow.

What she felt was like a huge, wet balloon, getting bigger and bigger, ready to explode. She didn't know what to do, kept seeing that girl getting slammed like a rag doll, kept seeing her dream with Paul swimming away.

She burst into tears. That lasted for some minutes, till she couldn't stand it anymore.

She called Beth.

"Hey!" came the bright voice immediately lifting her spirits. "How's it going? You good? Not so good? Good day, bad day?"

"Bad day." Liddy pulled a corner of the sheet to mop her face.

"No, what?" There was hubbub in the background.

"This isn't a good time for you."

"Never for you! Just another open house, same old, same old. What's wrong?"

In a weeping torrent Liddy poured it out…all of it heretofore unspoken: the trip to the police, the detective who'd gone to question Carl, the resulting stress with Paul.

"The police? Whoa. When did you go to the police?"

"Last week, I didn't want to worry you. *Don't let anyone hear you.*"

"They won't," Beth said low. "I'm out in the stairwell now."

"Oh…there's more." Liddy told about seeing the young woman get battered. "Bad enough, but…" She burst into new tears.

"But what, honey?"

"She looked like Sasha Perry. So either I'm right or I've gone completely off my rocker and need sympathy. Paul says it was probably just…s-some couple having a fight and that's what I get looking into someone's bedroom at three in the morning."

Hesitation at the other end; Beth was worrying.

"Paul *could* be right," she said dubiously. "But if there's anyone's gut I'd trust it would be yours before his or anybody's. Liddy dear, your husband's a not hugely deep, walking calculator, a living, breathing …I don't know…like one of those *machines* programmed only to work, and if you impede them they go all haywire, blow their fuses, send out sparks."

"When I saw that girl get slammed, I swear I wanted to call the police. Or that detective."

"What's her name?"

"Kerri Blasco."

"I saw her on television! She looks nice."

"I may still call her."

Thoughtful pause at the other end. "Wait," Beth said gently. "What you saw…*I've* been where that girl was, the awful fights before the divorce. It must happen a thousand times a night in this city."

"So do nothing?"

"Wait a little. Watch that building, and most of all, watch

116

yourself." Beth paused. "Save yourself, Lids. Most of all, save yourself. Something's going on, but you don't know what, so just…hang on. Pull it together and save yourself."

Silence from Liddy. She was mopping her face with the sheet. "You there? Lids?"

"I'm here. I may not sound it, but I feel better. Not ready to explode anymore. Thanks, Beth."

At the other end someone called to her. "*I'm coming,*" she called back. Then, to the phone, "Lids, you know how I almost once self-destructed, so please, do it for me. Put on the face, hang tight, and save yourself."

"Okay."

"And call if *anything*. Any time day or night - three in the morning, even!"

"Okay."

28.

She went to work. Forced herself like a nervous engine to finish the woman-in-rain watercolor - the easier job - and emailed the publisher that it was ready. Next she opened the window top to let out turpentine fumes, and sat on the tall stool to work on the Rawlie oil painting. Princess Whatsername's blue toga needed a thin, translucent glaze; in a rush Liddy mixed her palette's squeezed blob of cobalt blue with too much turpentine, made a smeary mess, lost patience and in a jerky movement knocked over her can full of brushes. Dammit, dammit! To cover the birch floor, they had ironically wound up putting down the same old tarp from the old apartment.

Good thing, because she'd also spilled some turpentine. Cursing, she knelt to clean.

Then went back to tackle the blue toga and finished Rawlie's post-apocalyptic light spear. She spent hours in a fervor, then packed it in, pulled the window's top sash closed and locked it, pushed Rawlie on his easel back into the corner, and went to shower again, knowing she reeked of turpentine.

She raised her face into the steaming downpour, feeling the warm, sedative pounding on her closed eyelids, her aching neck and shoulders. Her shampoo was lavender-scented and she scrubbed the soapy froth, replacing the turp smell with the intoxicating aroma of the sweetest herb on earth. It made her think of lavender fields in France - wide, stretching expanses of clearest blue leading up to old castles. Nice. The gloom that had dogged her all day was starting to ease.

Turning off the water, she looked over to the glass though

she'd promised herself she wouldn't. What was to fear? She'd showered this morning and there was nothing there.

She blinked. Her breath stopped in her throat.

There, right next to her at shoulder level, was the word *Help*. It looked written as if with a trembling finger and stayed there, not running down with the other droplets.

A quiet groan, almost of pain, escaped her lips. Involuntarily she backed up a step, shutting her eyes tight, opening them again.

It was still there.

Her head thudded crazily as she reached out to touch it, then pulled her hand back fast; reached hysterically up for a sponge and wiped the word away.

It stayed gone, but she still stood there, naked and shaking, feeling the dry rasp of her breath in her throat. She began to make a whining sound, unaware that she was making any sound at all.

"I WILL NOT BELIEVE THIS. NO…NOT HAPPENING…"

With a crazed, jerky movement she got out of the shower stall, slammed the door, grabbed a towel and wrapped it around her, tight, tighter, as if the towel could somehow hold her together. She stood like that for long, trembling moments, dread building until she could stand it no longer. She reached and yanked the shower door open again; looked in.

The *Help* was still gone, replaced by wild smears of soapy lather. Her eyes darted to the faucet, making dripping sounds that seemed abnormally loud. But that word was gone, and it stayed gone despite the humidity piling more hot mist on the glass.

Liddy dropped to the toilet seat. Sat there rigid for a long time, feeling the harsh breath in her throat finally slow.

"I've been tired for so long," she whispered out loud to herself, and it seemed okay, not crazy at all, to talk out loud like that. Her voice grew stronger. "So much has happened that I don't understand. The accident…these apparitions…everything." Then, slowly, she forced herself to stand, reach one hand to the sink for support.

"But it's all right. It's going to be all right. Beth says save yourself…"

She headed for the bedroom, still in her towel. Part of her mind pulled fearfully at her, tried to make her go compulsively back to check the shower – *no, dammit, nothing's there!* - but she went straight to her drawers instead; pulled out her prettiest underwear. Black lace bra and panties, just the thing to distract, think of nicer things. She had imagined what happened in the shower; she had imagined everything - that's right. It had been a bad three months…but it was over now. Her jaw clamped down hard. She was declaring war.

Put on the face, hang tight, save yourself.

I'm doin' it, Beth.

From the closet she pulled a simple black cotton dress, V-necked and sleeveless. It was one of Paul's favorites, he'd like that, though she decided to wear comfortable black flats to favor her bad leg. Next, putting on makeup before the mirror, she decided on an even better way to tackle this. If maybe she was actually losing her mind, well hey - she could still *fake* sanity, couldn't she? Mind over matter! Never again would she mention her hallucinations, or whatever they were, to anyone. Under extreme stress the mind plays cruel tricks. She'd been through a rough patch but it was over now. Finished. *Save yourself*, she thought urgently.

But bad stuff kept bubbling up. In the kitchen where she'd left her purse she remembered telling Alex Minton, "Those apparitions, it's like I'm seeing a ghost."

The thought sent her back to the studio for her sketchbook, which she pushed into her purse. She wasn't sure what she'd do with it at the restaurant, probably nothing, but she took it everywhere out of habit, didn't she? Ha - would she wave it around under Carl Finn's nose, see his reaction? Oh she was tempted, but that would be bad. Paul would get upset and it would be like last night all over again.

Peaceful was better. Paul looked so pleased announcing there'd be a surprise.

What surprise? The heart that wouldn't quit its cold thudding wasn't exactly feeling up for surprises.

Liddy stashed another lipstick in her purse, then locked the apartment and left.

Down in the street, in the still very warm waning sunlight, she stopped to look up to the window where she'd seen the fighting couple. For a long moment she stared at it, seeing again the pained, whirling-around face of the young blonde as he struck her. Terrible enough, but what shook Liddy even more was the feeling that wouldn't let go. That girl had looked like Sasha Perry - and what was she going to do about it? She had seen something that still tore at her, broke her heart, made her feel guilty.

Call, Kerri Blasco said. *If there's anything at all, don't hesitate.*

Wait, from Beth. *A thousand fights like that happen every night.*

And from Paul: *Stay away from the cops, they'll find noon at three o'clock!*

The window up there was quiet now, empty-looking with the shade pulled. Paul had to be right – it was some troubled couple who'd either made up or broken up, and she had built it up into-

Stop, Liddy stormed at herself. Down, crazy thoughts…

She exhaled, turned, and walked on, heading a block east and realizing that she was moving more briskly than she had in ages. That surprised her, made her smile. Ditto the sun, hot but not too hot and the good feeling being out in it, and seeing faces, people tired but glad to be heading home, bar doors open emitting laughter and music.

She turned north at Mercer, gazing ahead through the early-evening crowd…

…and her breath stopped.

There, crossing at mid-block and heading toward her, was Sasha Perry.

29.

Oh my God, no doubt this time, not a hallucination. Liddy's heart rocketed - it was her! The same girl who'd passed them at the sidewalk cafe, the long-haired blonde Liddy had sketched whose likeness shocked Beth *and* Kerri Blasco. My God, my God...

She was approaching, still wearing her black party dress with its bodice torn, her face crumpled in sadness as she watched the sidewalk beneath her feet. Liddy, gaping, saw bruises on her cheek near her right eye...she was getting closer...and then - oh my God, it was really her - she had her hair pulled back on one side and there was the Winnie the Pooh stud in her right ear. Liddy stood open-mouthed, her heart hammering. The girl passed her, practically brushed against her as she moved dully on.

"Sasha?" Liddy called. "Sasha Perry?" she called again, starting to follow.

The girl looked back, her features alarmed at hearing her name. She saw Liddy trailing her, limping a little, and she started to run.

"Please," Liddy begged, trying to move faster but she couldn't run, that was painful. Her breath came in harsh gasps as she forced herself anyway. *Move, feets!*

"Sasha, I want to help. I saw him hurt you..."

The girl was already across the intersection and heading west back on Prince. Liddy struggled to move faster; was suddenly sweating as she crossed too, calling *"I saw him hurt you,"* ducking a car honking, calling out to people on the other side. "Please, stop that girl, I just want to help her!"

Some turned toward where she was pointing, then looked confused or indifferent. Another crazy. Liddy reached the sidewalk, peering frantically from their faces to where Sasha was…and suddenly wasn't. She was gone, blended into the crowd before the building of the fighting couple.

Had she gone in or run past? No telling; there were people in the way. Sasha had disappeared, and Liddy, gasping for breath, was getting looks.

"You okay?" one man cuddling his Yorkie stopped to ask her.

"Yes, thanks," she managed between gasps, sweating and hurting. How long since she'd moved even half that fast?

Breathing hard raised all kinds of alarm in hip, healthy Soho. The man and then a woman coming up behind him started suggesting gyms in the area, commenting on how important it was to stay in shape. The woman even asked would she like something to drink? A chair to sit in? She started pulling a chair up from a near sidewalk café.

Liddy raised her hand no, they were too kind she told them, still panting as she stepped under an awning's shadow. Now the man wanted to know why she was calling *I saw him hurt you.*

"Is someone in trouble?" he asked; and the woman and then a second woman coming up started piping, "Call the police! If you think someone's in trouble call the cops!"

"If you think someone's…"

Had they *not* seen a girl running – an eye catching, hair-flying blonde with a bruised face and torn party dress? It was hot; nobody ran in this heat. Nobody went tearing across a busy intersection with horns honking without being noticed.

Except me, Liddy realized, feeling her stomach drop. They only saw me.

"I must have been mistaken," she stammered. "Thanks again."

She got funny looks as they left.

Confused and frightened, she stood staring at the place where she'd last seen the fleeing Sasha…in front of the building across from their loft.

Finally she turned, faced again the intersection of Prince and Mercer. She cringed, hearing herself calling out again like a crazy woman.

The wild dash had left her leg throbbing, but she trudged, dreading the six blocks between there and the restaurant.

30.

She got more funny looks when she arrived. "I know, I'm a sweaty mess," she said, feeling light-headed as both men rose – Paul with a questioning expression, Carl, his smile dazzling and too jovial by a mile, introducing her to his new girlfriend, giggling Nicki in spaghetti straps and a deep, *deep* V-neck.

"You should have cabbed it," Paul frowned, concerned.

"Six blocks?" Liddy sat and deep-breathed as Carl, who looked as if he'd already had a few, jokingly asked if she'd taken the sweatshop route, and Nicki told her importantly that she was studying sweatshops in the new global economy.

Liddy smiled. "I saw right away how serious you are."

A waiter came. The others ordered new rounds of martinis. Liddy nixed alcohol because she still felt light-headed.

The place was air-conditioned, at least, and a tall, cold Coke helped to revive although the leg still hurt. The new martinis arrived, and they all got down to the serious business of socializing - which Liddy loathed even when things weren't terrible. Socializing means you have to *talk,* smile sweetly at the guy opposite you who last night your husband said blamed you because the cops bothered him. But no sign of animosity now from across the table; she put on the face and beamed as Carl toasted their "new adventure in their great new apartment," and there were smiles and pleasantries all around. Carl's current squeeze was right out of the cookie cutter: young and pretty, a shiny bright undergrad who couldn't keep her hands off him. He'd worn a blazer over one of his many pastel polo shirts, and her hand kept going under the blazer, patting his chest, his heart, his tummy after she fed him some antipasto in an endive leaf.

"Ooh, crunchy, isn't it?" Nicki giggled. They were so into each other that Paul had the chance for an aside to Liddy.

He slugged his drink first, then leaned to her. "Why'd you look like you crawled through the desert when you got here?"

"It was hot." She avoided his gaze.

"Not that hot." She felt him grin. "You chase one of your ghosts or something?"

It occurred in that moment that Paul was a jerk - maybe the word's smartest dumb, insensitive jerk. Pity you can't haul off and smack someone in a nice, sedate place like this, so Liddy's belly just clenched as she studied her Coke.

"Lemme guess," Paul pressed, feeling his booze. "I'll bet you crossed to that building where you saw the fighting couple. Tried to climb the fire escape or something."

"Stop."

"Or - you went looking for that girl, that's it."

"I said stop."

She hissed it, but it still came out too loud, interrupting Carl and Nicki who looked up from the menu they'd been cuddling into.

"Trouble in paradise?" Carl asked, raising his eyebrows.

"Yeah." Paul's lips curled slightly. "Liddy's been seeing a ghost."

"Ooh," Nicki cooed. "I love ghost stories! Can I see the ghost too?"

"Maybe." It came out with just a tinge of sarcasm, but Liddy was furious that Paul would make light of what to her was still traumatic. He was so clueless he hadn't even noticed her anger; had turned away and was suddenly deep in conversation with Carl who was yakking excitedly about rat brains. Well, fine! Since they weren't looking her way – and Nicki was, expectantly - she subtly reached to her purse and pulled out her sketchbook; opened to the page, kept the sketchbook between them and below the linen table edge, and showed it.

"I saw her in the street and sketched her," she told Nicki. "Now I'm told she's the missing coed Sasha Perry."

I just drew her, not the same as saying I saw a ghost. Carl and Paul were now going on about blocked rodent receptor sites as Nicki leaned closer…gave the sketch a double take.

"Wow, Sasha Perry, I recognize her from the news," she said in a low oh gee voice, and looked back up to Liddy. "You *are* good - and you *saw* her?"

"Well, someone who apparently looks like her." Still deflecting, but feeling her heart lurch remembering the running blond girl – *it was Sasha* - the Winnie the Pooh stud in her right ear, a detail Kerri said hadn't been in any released photos. Too bad, Liddy decided, if no one else on Prince Street saw her; she wanted to jump up right now and call Kerri, but she couldn't. Paul had just glanced at her briefly and Nicki was ogling the sketch Liddy still held low – then seconds later the waiter returned with salads. Attention was diverted to ordering main courses and the waiter filling the four wine glasses, and Liddy hurried her sketchbook back to her purse. Angry or not, she'd suddenly felt uptight about having it out. Really, she told herself: sleeping dogs, thin ice, keep the fragile peace, maybe take her phone to the ladies room?

The Coke and air-conditioning had restored, and the glass of wine before her looked good. Liddy drank; let it go down, start to work. Ah, better. Nicki was sipping her wine too, listing in her chair a little.

"Finish my martini?" Nicki asked, pushing her half full glass to Liddy. "I had two at the bar before this one, I feel dizzy."

Liddy thanked, finished Nicki's martini, and slugged more wine. Paul gave her a slight frown. She gave him a go to hell look.

They were all digging into their salads when Nicki turned to Carl. "You knew Sasha Perry, didn't you?"

Liddy's fork stopped halfway to her mouth. The light-headedness from her wild chase was replaced by the effects of the booze, and she wasn't sure she'd heard right. Paul stared as Nicki dove into Liddy's purse for her sketchbook and pulled it up and pushed it at Carl, who looked quickly away from it and said no, he'd never laid eyes on the girl, and Nicki insisted, "But wasn't she in your biochem class? No wait - she only *audited* – a friend of a friend knew her and said so."

Liddy blinked as last night flashed - Paul stressing about Carl's pique, blaming her. *He'd told Kerri he didn't know Sasha.*

Tension all around: Carl started to argue with Nicki; Liddy stashed her sketchbook back while Paul helped bury the subject under a tide of thin witticisms about everyone seeing this girl's ghost. Carl glared, Paul switched to shop talk, and Nicki was easily distracted; felt terrible hearing about adorable little white mice who'd been sacrificed in their experiments – but they hadn't felt a thing, promise. Just went to sleep high and happy, not so good for us, ha.

Then Paul saw Liddy staring at Carl; caught her eye: *Stop, means nothing.* She looked away; *Oh yeah?*

"Can I join the fun?" she heard, and looked up into the pale eyes of Ben Allen standing there, flushed and grinning expectantly from Carl to Paul. "You tell yet?"

How relieved they both looked at the distraction, trading grins that instantly forgot the last few minutes.

What now? Liddy thought.

"The surprise," Paul said brightly, inviting Ben to sit. Ben pulled up two chairs from a table just vacated as his date named Amber joined them. "Hi!" said Amber. "We've been at the bar!"

Then, as if announcing that they'd found the cure for cancer, Paul beamed again. "The boat," he said, leaning to Liddy. "Carl and Ben are going to buy it. Joint venture."

Amber started gushing about how thrilled she was, she'd always wanted to learn sailing, and Ben said he was looking forward to losing his New York pallor, get back out in the sun and the wind. He looked excited until he saw Liddy's expression; looked to Paul, then looked back to Liddy. "You didn't know?"

Paul told her quickly that they'd just decided yesterday. "*Firmly*, I mean. We've been talking about it for a while."

They were all a blur. The last few minutes' chatter had been like white noise to Liddy, replaying instead what she'd heard about Carl and Sasha. She didn't care about the boat. "It's Paul's," she told Ben after a beat. "I knew it would sell sooner or later."

Paul reached for her hand and squeezed it. "Hey, we're nearly flush. Is that a surprise or what? You happy?"

She smiled and nodded; pulled her hand away.

He was disappointed. "You don't seem happy."

"It's not that. My leg hurts."

"We'll cab home."

"Fine."

Ben leaned closer to Liddy, oblivious to someone squeezing past behind his chair. "This changes nothing," he said feelingly. His dark hair was slicked back, his pale eyes earnest. "We'll still *all* of us go out, have good times like always but this way" – his glance flicked to Carl, who smirked – "we won't have to feel guilty about borrowing the boat so much."

He was more white noise, just babbling his practiced sincerity.

Liddy was staring at Carl.

Barely joined the others saying 'bye to Ben as he rose, gave a slightly drunken salute – squint: *Gilligan's Island* – then left with Amber, who waved amid lots of "Ship ahoy!" and "nice meeting you!"

Carl's watch seemed to startle him. "The time!" he said, and clapped Paul's arm. "We gotta jet. Lab awaits."

Paul looked back from sizing up Liddy, and shook his head. "I think I've had too much to drink. I'll catch up tomorrow."

That started another fuss: But that still-alive mouse - they had to test her before she croaked!

While they were at it, Liddy subtly asked Nicki for her phone number, saying she wanted to hear more about sweatshops in the global economy. For a second she thought Paul saw her. She wasn't sure.

Two cabs were hailed in the street, Nicki dispatched into one, Liddy and Paul climbing into the other.

Neither of them spoke as the cab pulled away.

31.

Alex sat, his hands around the steering wheel, his eyes moving from a glance through the windshield to another into the rear-view mirror. It was ridiculous – the street was so dark you couldn't see anything no matter where you looked; with its kind of inhabitants, what chance did a light bulb have?

"Nothing," he muttered.

"Wait," Kerri said.

Muffled transmissions resumed from Gini Tang's transmitter, the tiny, third button down in the Vice cop's see-through blouse.

"Ooh, you *are* my kind of man, such *muscles*," she giggled, sounding drunk which she wasn't; she'd faked it when Ray Gruner picked her up.

"Five blocks," they heard Buck Dillon whisper, positioned at the rear of the decrepit second floor where Gini was headed with her hookup. The button in her blouse also contained a GPS.

Kerri concentrated on her earpiece; fiddled a stray strand of hair back into her pony tail.

"Jo?" Alex said to his shoulder.

"We're good," whispered Jo Babiak, positioned behind the slum, hunched by trash cans opposite the fire escape to block Gruner's escape. She had uniforms with her. SWAT guys too.

Kerri let out a huge, pent-up breath. This was painful, this time it had to be perfect. It had looked good eleven days ago when they caught Ray Gruner - and then the slime slithered free on a technicality! She worried, she was frantic. It had to go right this time, if not tonight, she feared they'd never get him. The sadist who enjoyed raping and brutally beating his victims to death was also smart. Had lain low; controlled his kill-addiction for a whole eleven nights and even sent a smirk to plain clothes cops tailing him. Alternate pairs had shadowed his every move and he'd had fun taunting them: chatting nicely to the girl in the pizza place, spending his days in his dump, emerging only briefly to buy a newspaper, sit on a bench faking reading while, behind his shades, those narrow eyes watched every woman go by. Tonight was the first night he'd gone out. Cop radios were alerted. Gruner's addiction had finally overpowered him and he'd resumed his prowl.

"Four blocks." Buck's hushed whisper.

"Got it," Alex answered.

He and Kerri tensed, listening to Gini dicker with Gruner about her price. "Two hundred?" he argued. "I can get it for less."

"Not what *I* can give you - oh baby, you ain't seen shit till you see what *I* can give you."

Gruner wanted his kill so he faked relenting. They bargained, moving slowly. Gini's faked drunkenness was her excuse to dawdle; gave the cops time to move in.

Alex inhaled. "So finish about Sasha," he said. "We've got maybe three minutes."

"That's it," Kerri said morosely. "I've hit a dead end." She watched a homeless man shamble by. Under his rags and long, greasy wig she knew it was another cop. "Carl Finn said he never laid eyes on her, and I can't find anything that proves he did, not in student registration or canvassing the campus in my free time. In one bar some kid *thought* he saw her coming out of one of Finn's classes, but he was stoned that day. Memory's foggy."

"But Finn's the guy in Becca's selfie?"

"Definitely. I blew the pic way up and compared it to him in person. It's him."

Alex grunted. "Circumstantial even if it is."

"Like I said, I hit a dead end."

132

The homeless guy with a Glock under his rags had stopped near their car; turned, shuffled back before the darkened stoop. Kerri bit her lip, watching him, watching two other cops further down, dressed like dealers. They had practically an armed camp around them. Another miss at Gruner would be it; he'd run to another state; disappear briefly, then kill again.

They listened through another transmission – the rapist was getting impatient and they were moving faster, a block away now – no…less than a block.

"But you still like Finn for this?" Alex asked. "Despite the selfie's circumstantial…"

"I just wish I could tie him-"

"They're here," Alex said.

Out of the darkness, suddenly, came Tang and Gruner, Tang in her tight shorts laughing, teasing, pulling him up the crumbling stoop past the watching, hunched cop in his rags. All transmissions stilled; breaths held. What came from Gini Tang determined what next to the split second. Their shuffling sounded on the creaking stairs. Gini's key in the door rattled. "Shitty old locks," she giggled; then: "Enter," she said grandly, throwing the door open as planned; then: "Wait, mind if I check what you got? I'm discerning too, ya know." She grabbed his genitals as planned; then: "Oh, you're so *small* - hey, call *that* a hard on?"

"Ow!" Gruner yelled in pain. "You bitch!"

Sounds of thudding. Muffled cries trying to scream over obscenities and the sound of struggling, dragging, the door slammed-

But they were out. Up the stoop with their guns up, the cop in rags behind them, joining Buck already kicking the door down, bursting in on big, muscled Ray Gruner on little Gini Tang throttling her, so crazed that if he heard them he didn't stop, he had one massive hand on her throat and his other fist raised to smash her face-

133

-only Buck caught it, Gruner's fist, and Alex and Buck wrestled him off, face down on the floor with Alex's knee in his back, one hand holding his Glock to Gruner's head while Buck got Gruner's other arm behind him.

Yelling, writhing, the three struggled as Kerri kneeled in and got cuffs on him. "Give it up, shithead," she yelled; then Alex roared, "You are under arrest. You have the right to remain silent. Anything you say..."

They'd recorded him, and Gini's tiny button's infra red had recorded the attack. This time there'd be no slip-up, no slithering free of the system like when they hadn't gotten him to *speak*.

Lights were on, other cops were running in, and Alex pressed Gruner's face hard to the floor; banged it for good measure. He wanted more; they all wanted more. He bellowed, "Do you understand the rights I've just read to you?"

No answer. Yelling and writhing but not what they needed. Gini was on her knees with Kerri holding her. Alex lifted Gruner's head by his hair, bashed his face down harder. *"Do you understand what I've just read to you?"* he roared.

From the floor came a small, spreading pool of blood from Gruner's nose. He turned his head to the side; glared at Gini; glared at Kerri.

"Yeth," he growled because he'd lost a tooth; and then, "You're *hurting* me."

They had him. It was over, witnessed, caught on cop cam and recorded.

More cops arrived. EMTs too but Gruner could walk, they told them, so the EMTs just wiped and stuffed Gruner's bloody nose. Buck and Alex yanked him up by his cuffs behind him like a side of beef, and he howled.

"Fuckin' police *brutality*," he whined, and bitched and whined more as they dragged him down the stairs and out.

32.

When the cab pulled away, Paul stood staring at the building across the way.

"Fess up," he said quietly. "You think you saw that girl."

"Right," Liddy snapped, heading for the door. "She's grown angel wings and flown away. Can we go in, please?"

Paul persisted, following up the stairs that were painful for her. "You arrived looking like you'd seen a ghost. And that *glare* you gave Carl – you embarrassed *me*."

"Why do you always protect him?" Liddy stormed up, not turning.

"Because he has nothing to do with this…*obsession* of yours."

"You said he told the cops he didn't know Sasha."

"That's what he told me! Why wouldn't I believe him?"

"It's just kind of interesting, isn't it? That she was in his class?"

"You believe that from a pinhead?"

"You saw how fast he looked away from the sketch - and Sasha only *audited*, that's why there's no record."

They'd reached their landing. Paul threw his hands up and gestured helplessly as they approached their door. "We made this great move that was supposed to help, and you've gotten more..."

"More what?" Through clenched teeth.

"More…like you need more visits to Minton."

"Maybe *you* should go to Minton. *Denial for the sake of ambition, huh?*"

Enough. Liddy's hands shook and she just wanted to get away from Paul, be alone. He was overdoing his I-give-up tack, standing there sighing and hunched and miserable – it just added to her fury, so she fished in her purse and snapped, "*Okay*, I saw Sasha Perry."

He looked at her; blinked. "You couldn't have." His tone was flat, frightened.

"Right! So either she's alive or I'm crazy and saw a ghost. You happy?"

She raised her hand to key open the door...and it popped open. Then creaked opened further.

Liddy stared. Her eyes darted from the door's lock to its handle to the sliver of dark interior beyond. She heard Paul's breath catch.

"I locked this," she whispered, feeling chilled.

"Liddy."

"I locked it, I remember distinctly."

She knew he was thinking, *Right, like you saw Sasha Perry.*

"Wait here," he said raggedly.

With a jerky movement he pushed in, leaving the door open. Liddy peered fearfully into the interior, seeing him turn on lamps, cross the loft's open expanse to the bedroom and the other rooms. She was stunned, not believing this, her anger collapsing as she plunged back into self-doubt. Her eyes flew back to the lock, the new one they'd replaced for the old one, and she shook her head.

"Locked it," escaped thinly from her lips, sounding like the soft mewling of a child.

Paul was back. "Nothing." He pointed unhappily to the security keypad. "You didn't set this either?"

Either. Hurtful word, saying she was out of it.

"That I forgot" – her voice shook – "but I clearly remember locking the door." Something that had felt full of strong and righteous anger minutes before was gone, plowed under. She felt incredulous and beaten; let him take her arm and lead her in, closing and locking the door, punching the security pad. Everything from the last few hours came back and she questioned it…like the *Help* in the shower wall mist, and seeing Sasha in the street - had any of it really happened? No one else saw Sasha…so had she, Liddy, gone truly crazy, paranoid, seeing and imagining things?

Paul had left her standing in the middle of the room and dropped, miserable, to the couch with his back to her, facing the flat screen. A lamp by his side glowed softly. It was the Victorian glass lamp Liddy had bought just days before, and it hurt, remembering how buoyant she had felt. Now the awful pent-up feeling was back, like a large, pressing hand over her heart.

What to do with this pain? Go into her studio and lock the door? Lie down on the window seat, try to decompress?

Possible. He wouldn't bother her, but she knew she'd still feel wretched.

Like a dummy he sat. From the back he looked dead, almost, as if someone had just left him there, propped him up with his head drooping.

Her turmoil was giving way to guilt. One thing about Paul: if they fought and she relented first, he'd come around and they'd both feel better. Touch brows, say sorry. In a way, Paul was emotionally like her mirror. He took his cues from her…same as he took his cues from Carl. His problem was that he was too malleable. Liddy saw what he didn't, but he was still caught in the middle.

She came, took a deep breath, and sat stiffly next to him. His arms were folded and he stared at nothing, looking ill. It was depressingly quiet in the apartment. Now the two of them must have looked like dummies, staring glassily ahead at the blank flat screen.

"Sorry," she said, biting back a last, stubborn chip of anger.

He inhaled. Let a long moment pass, then said, "Me too."

She fell back on the cushions, glad, at least, to feel her heart start to slow.

More silence passed between them. Finally, very quietly, Paul said, "Please go back to Minton."

"I never stopped."

"You cut from twice a week to once a week."

She realized then why she'd sat next to him. Something strong inside her was back, announcing it was still *there* – fighting. "He's useless. Just gives me pills, talks and talks and says nothing."

"Some of that talk might be useful."

She felt it: Paul's turmoil still coming off him in waves. Still looking ahead, he said in that same quiet voice, "You really think you saw that girl?"

Liddy took a deep breath. "Yes."

"In the neighborhood?"

"Yes. Running away from me."

"Out of the whole city you think you saw her here."

"She went to NYU. Here or the Village would be logical."

Paul hesitated; glanced uneasily over to Charlie Bass's plants. "Been spraying 'em?"

"Yes."

"Seeing any apparitions? Blond girl's faces?"

"Not in two days." It was true, and no way was Liddy going to mention seeing the word *Help* hours earlier in the steamy shower stall. The something strong in her was kicking harder, straining to pull her back up.

Paul's arm went to the end table beside him. Under the Victorian glass lamp he found the DVD of Charlie Bass's *Vampire Island*.

"What's this?"

"Bought it for a lark." She wanted to sound confident; saw again her exchange with the friendly young assistant at Pete's Old Books, and the memory cheered her. "See? No fear here of things that go bump in the night." Paul looked worriedly at her, so she added, figuring any kind of talk helped ease further tension, "In the store they said the movie's sweet, actually - and sad. Charlie played a guy who didn't want to be a vampire, but he was surrounded, threatened. Showed his talent in his struggle against onrushing tragedy."

The change of subject seemed to work a little. If all else failed, even a lousy cable show was better than this silence.

"Let's see." Paul rose slowly, stiffly, went to the flat screen, pushed in the DVD and started it.

Liddy turned off the lamp and they watched. A glowing distance shot of some desert island came into view as music swelled; then there was Charlie, lying wet on a beach like a castaway just washed to shore. Credits rolled. A stranger approached, friendly and concerned-looking – *kinda like Ben Allen*, Liddy caught herself thinking and squashed it, her heart hurting from negativity.

"I googled the movie," she said, trying to keep up her lame patter. "Charlie lost thirty pounds filming it."

Paul shifted and said nothing, his face still tight in the dimness.

Charlie was hungry? asked the stranger on the beach. Come meet our hostages. Hostages? Ten minutes in Charlie found out what that meant and was horrified. Fifteen minutes in someone jumped him, and in a scene of horrible, bloody struggle sank his fangs into Charlie's neck. He was now a vampire too - but a good vampire, protesting, begging. He escaped and tried to hide but they were everywhere and he was starving, worse and worse, his face going skull-like with dark, sickly shadows under his eyes, literally wasting away on the screen. He begged and pleaded…

…and Paul got up. "It's stupid," he said, going to the window.

Liddy exhaled in defeat. Nice try. He was still seriously upset and - face it, she thought; we both are.

Now what?

She switched off the movie, couldn't stand the silence, turned on the TV. The news was on. Excited coverage of a dark, floodlit street blazing with police and emergency vehicles, the voiceover describing the stunning capture of terrifying serial rapist and killer, Ray Gruner. Then came a close up, and Liddy caught her breath at the familiar face and swinging blond ponytail helping get Gruner into a police car. The camera tightened its focus on the alert, pretty face as the voiceover said, "...Detective Kerri Blasco, instrumental in building the months-long case against Gruner, also in the news as the only police officer still investigating the case of missing coed, Sasha Perry."

Paul turned from staring out the window. "Blasco," he said dismally. "Your friend?"

Liddy blinked at the screen, feeling a *ping* of joy as she remembered Kerri smiling, listening kindly that night in the police station; remembered too their conversation when she'd called to identify Sasha's ear stud. She'd been upset and crying. Kerri had been comforting, had taken time, reassured her.

Call if anything, she said.

Right now this second, Liddy wanted to run into the studio or the bathroom, lock the door and call her, tell her about seeing Sasha just three hours ago. Her heart started pounding...she was bursting to call...and then she stopped, remembering that no one else seemed to have seen Sasha; remembering too the damned front door she could have sworn she'd locked...and hadn't because there it was again, before her eyes popping open at just a touch, creaking further open into darkness...

Self doubt tore at her. Push to remember more, she decided, some further detail - maybe even sleep on it, let the wine and Nicki's martini finish wearing off. They were crazy busy now anyway, the cops. Calling could wait...

The news had switched to a pet food commercial.

Liddy switched off the TV, turned the small lamp back on, and went to Paul.

33.

Jubilation! The place sounded like the roof was going to blow off, with voices pitched high and glasses clinking and odd bursts of laughter penetrating the general commotion. They were at Haley's Bar, on West 45th, with more cops and reporters still running in, the reporters squeezing through with their cameras and asking how did it feel, this great success?

Bleeping bleeping *great,* they got with grins over and over – okay, edits required - but the pictures would still look fantastic on the morning news after they re-ran the blazing night scene of Gruner's capture. Reporters looked around for more celebrants to interview. A lot of them were still watching the overhead TVs, but they'd seen it before, cable was running the capture non-stop, and they went back to their cheers and hugging and back-slapping. Oh, this was fun.

Pushing her way to the bar, Kerri waved to various members of her team. Pints were raised to her. Alex slid his beer to her and she raised his glass back. A female reporter reached her, thrust out her mike and asked excitedly how she felt. Kerri's flushed face turned thoughtful.

"We're all relieved, naturally," she said, giving Alex back his pint. He turned from the reporter to talk to Buck Dillon and Jo Babiak. "My team," Kerri intoned, "and over fifty members of the police force worked hard." She hesitated. "We'd like to think the city is now a safer place, and it is but there's always more. There are so many crimes."

"Speaking of which," the reporter pressed - she was caked with makeup and loud – "You are the last officer to devote your personal time to the Sasha Perry case. Have you made any progress there?"

"'Fraid I can't comment, thank you," Kerry said, politely dismissing, turning back to Alex and the others. A few minutes of glad, weary exchange passed between them, then Jo Babiak glanced out to the crowd and said, "Hey, Hank's here."

Happy Henry Kubic, the bespectacled FBI psychiatrist who'd done a profile for them on Gruner and others; had really nailed Gruner's *addiction* to killing and its timing, predicting he'd be unable to go much more than eight or nine days before resuming his prowl. Kerri normally didn't place much stock in FBI profilers – they were often way off – but Hank was good. He had intuition on top of his science; Kerri believed in intuition.

He was in a blue shirt and jeans talking with two off-duty detectives from the sixth precinct. She went to him; got hugs from both cops who waved and peeled off, then another big, embarrassing *squeeze* from Hank Kubic.

"Congrats, I'm so happy," he said, grinning behind his wire rims. "Couldn't stay away especially 'cause I've got something for you."

"Oh?"

Another reporter was bugging Kerri so she ignored and suggested they find a quiet place. They did, in a booth way at the end where the crowd was thinner.

"Tell," she said, sliding in, facing him. The flameless candle between them didn't throw much light. Silverware for two and checkered cloth napkins filled a mason jar.

From his breast pocket he'd already pulled folded papers and was spreading them. "Sorry it's been crazy, I finally got the chance to look at Liddy Barron – what you know about her, anyway. This is *something*. There's a few red flags here."

He looked like Jiminy Cricket, Hank did, and when something excited or fascinated him, his small frame nearly bounced around in enthusiasm. Months ago they had a different killer about to get off on a technicality, and Hank had gone off on what seemed like an annoying tangent about the creep's hatred of shoelaces – and then: "He fears confinement! Shut him in a closet!" Minutes later the slime was screaming to get out, screaming he'd tell where he'd buried the bodies, hidden his gun. Now Hank was pointing and tapping on his papers and starting to spew about Shakespeare and Dostoyevsky, then excusing himself, saying he should back up, start from the beginning.

"You wanted to know the possibility, just the possibility, right?"

"Actually it wasn't me, it was Mackey's suggestion – read, order. Our dear lieutenant's been getting worried and frustrated with me, says I look too tired, says he heard I nearly keeled over at last Wednesday's deposition."

"Ah, hence the request I look at this?"

Kerri nodded. Hank nodded too and went back to his papers.

"Hallucinations and nightmares can come from a person's *own guilt*. I'm not saying this is Liddy Barron – neither of us knows enough – it's just something you should consider."

Kerri stared at his clipped, upside down report: several pages, longer than she'd dreamed he'd make, especially since he'd volunteered his time.

"You're saying," she frowned slightly, "that the person *reporting* the torment of nightmares etc. could be the bad guy?"

"It happens." Hank rotated his papers so she could read them. "Case histories compared with Liddy Barron's. Again I can't say identical or even close because neither of us knows enough."

He knew Kerri could both read and listen, so he continued.

"She came to you, right?"

"Yes. Out of the blue."

"So a cry for help or attention - or…" He hesitated. "A *confession*, the beginning anyway."

143

Kerri looked up from his notes.

"In describing her nightmares, they all involved water?"

"Yes."

"No PTSD stuff at all about her car accident?"

"No."

Hank grunted; then counted off items one by one on his fingers. "That photo Sasha sent her friend of the Hudson, combined with the fact that the Barron boat is kept at the 79th Street docks near where that photo was taken, combined with these water images Liddy described to you - *wanted* to tell you about..."

"Also wanted to show her Sasha sketch, said she wasn't sure she'd ever even seen her, wanted me to know that too."

"Yes...yes..." Hank's fingers drummed. "Wow."

He leaned forward. "Here's the thing: Say someone in the heat of a terrible moment does something so horrible that the memory must repress it...but it *can't* – that's what makes us human, the psyche really can't force out memories too awful to face, so they come out sideways - as other things that are easier to deal with like ghosts or hallucinations or *anything* scary that's socially okay to complain about."

Kerri stared at the flameless candle, listening, taking it in as Hank pulled the silverware-stuffed mason jar to him and raced back to Shakespeare.

"The best psychiatrist *ever*, better than Freud, Shakespeare was. Consider Macbeth, a seriously screwed-up guy, weak, insecure, jealous, wants to kill the king so he can be king."

"One semester of English lit, I remember. Macbeth wanted to be king of Scotland."

"Right, only he's a terrified weenie, so his scheming, ambitious wife Lady Macbeth pushes and goads him so even *before* he kills he's so pressured - starting to go nuts - that he starts seeing hallucinations." Hank pulled a steak knife from the mason jar's napkin. "*Is this a dagger I see before me?*" Hank waved his knife wildly. "Poor Mac really thinks he's seeing it! Then he has to kill Banquo, his former best friend, fellow general and sudden rival" – Hank jerked the knife past his throat – "so next it's Banquo's ghost he thinks he sees and freaks out, embarrasses his wife who tells their freaked-out dinner guests he's just having a fit, an illness. But they *both* go bonkers – the whole play's really about *insanity* – remember Lady Macbeth sleepwalking and hallucinating about blood on her hands? *Out, damn spot!* Whew - the best description of paranoia anywhere and it was done by Shakespeare in 1609! Unless you count Dostoyevsky's *Crime and Punishment* where Raskolnikov sees the ghost of the woman he murdered laughing at him, driving him crazy..."

"I get it." Kerri was nodding. "Guilt still spills out."

"It splinters the mind. Both Macbeth and his missus slip into madness and hallucinations – see terror that isn't there." Hank started re-rolling his knife into its checkered napkin. "So how does this apply to your case?" He leaned forward with his eyebrows up. "*I don't know.* Just wanted you to see the big picture. The mind is a crazy thing."

"I'll say."

He handed her his several-page printout. "For you. Fascinating cases, several parallels to this one."

Kerri shook her head, picturing Liddy Barron looking so lost and scared that night she came to the squad room. "I hope none of this applies."

"Ditto. What are you going to do now?"

"I don't know. Think hard." Kerri started putting the papers into her bag.

"Maybe just call her. Ask how she's feeling."

"I thought of that."

"If you do, ask her about sleepwalking. Seeing dead people."

34.

Paul was standing with his back to her, looking out. Coming closer, Liddy saw his gaze shift from the building across the way to somewhere down the street. Neither of them spoke. He wore the same troubled look he'd worn since they'd come back to the apartment.

Something was off here. Liddy frowned, looking out, sifting through everything that had happened in this whole, awful night. Something nagged, and she realized it had been nagging from the moment they left the restaurant. She looked back to Paul, wanting to gauge his reaction.

"Why did you tell Carl you'd had too much to drink and couldn't work tonight?"

His gaze in profile froze. Below, dimly, there was a screech of brakes and someone screamed, but Paul seemed not to notice. Liddy checked. They were okay down there. Up here…

She took a deep breath and her heart speeded up. A feeling of anger too, growing, coming back.

"You're really, seriously worried because we now know Sasha Perry was Carl's student. That's what's troubling you, isn't it? You're afraid I'll – what? Run to the police?"

"No," he said softly, but didn't look at her.

"And if Carl had anything – *anything* – to do with Sasha's disappearance, that would be bad for you, right?"

"Bad for us, Lids."

"Investigations would torpedo your paired triumph." Her voice shook. "Not just the money but the fame, your name in the science journals – what you've struggled for all your life *even*

146

if there's something behind it that's making your wife crazy."

"No, for God's sake."

"What then?" She started to cry.

It came out slowly, in that same soft, sorry voice. "I've always sensed…known, really…that you resented my relationship with Carl. That on some level you were…jealous."

Liddy gaped at him. "You're not serious."

"You've never liked him. You resent that we've been friends for over twenty years."

"No, you *haven't*. You both lost touch for *years* - only resumed for the research."

"Carl has helped me more than you know."

"He's *used* you – ever since you were his boat boy - and *nothing's changed.*" A tear slid to the corner of Liddy's mouth. "Sure, he had the Big Pharma connections and got you on board-"

"He could have asked someone else."

"Oh, but he had his" – she made desperate air quotes – "working relationship with you from way back. *Tally the day's notes, Paul, wouldja? Hey, Paul, I'm bushed, would you do the week's accounting?* Do you not see? Are you still that poor boy saying Oh thanks for letting me scrub your boat, Carl?"

Paul hung his head. Long, wrenching moments passed; then, like a limp balloon refilling, he raised his head again.

She was surprised. In profile she saw tears brimming his large, pleading eyes; his head shook back and forth as if trying to ward off an emotional storm. "This isn't about Carl," he half choked. "It's…you. I'm just so…scared of what's going on with you. I've tried everything, I don't know what to do."

"Don't change the subject!"

"You *are* the subject. You've become obsessed with this missing girl – and now because you dislike Carl you've seized on some connection to him because of something his drunk date said - but you're not making sense." Paul inhaled raggedly. "You've also said you've *seen* her, which means she's *alive* and maybe hiding for some damned reason-"

"From *him*." Liddy floundered and raised her hands helplessly. "She'd been in drug trouble. Carl's an M.D. who can prescribe and...I don't know, maybe he's been *dealing* – and maybe a romance too and she got demanding and threatened to tell..." A terrible thought hit. "Oh Paul," Liddy breathed, her eyes sorrowful. "Even if you suspected him...you'd still cover for him, wouldn't you?"

"*Stop*, this is paranoid, oh God...I can't..." He threw his arms up, then turned and almost fell into her arms, making her stagger back with his weight. His chest pulled in a convulsive gasp that was expelled in a racking sob.

Liddy held him, anger dissolving as she felt a new sense of alarm. Now it was him going to pieces? He couldn't speak. His sobs were heavy and he clung to her, his face on her shoulder, almost crushing the wind from her.

"We're going in circles." She found herself consoling, becoming more alarmed as the awful thought came to her: *just who here is crazy?*

At last his sobs became words, incoherent at first, but clearer as his tears began to slow.

"...just want us...the way we were. We had every...dream and I want that back. Please, Lids. Don't damage. Don't destroy."

Her breath stopped. Like last night? she thought. Let sleeping dogs lie, in other words? The thought cut her, like something cold and sharp.

He straightened, his weight coming off her, his frantic eyes searching hers. "Promise me you'll get better, and everything will be...good, I beg you."

She returned his gaze wearily, without a smile. "We're tired, not thinking straight," she said. "Come to bed."

She led him, like a child. He was limp from emotion. She made hushing sounds as she helped him to bed, got into a nightgown, climbed in too.

His eyes were squeezed shut before she turned off the light. After she did, his voice came to her, weakly. "That thing about Carl is crazy, don't believe it..."

Because he didn't want to believe it.

Liddy said nothing, again seeing Nicki pushing Sasha's sketch at Carl as he practically ducked it bleating no, no, he'd never seen the girl, and Nicki insisted, "But she only *audited* your class – a friend of a friend said so."

Audited meant there'd be no record. That's how Carl so easily dodged Kerri.

"You'll see Minton again?" Paul's plaintive voice again. "Twice a week?"

Liddy's fists tightened. "He's useless. If I say *nothing* he takes notes. I need every minute to catch up on work."

"Please?"

She sighed, too worn out with her mind blown, knowing that only placating would get this to end. "Maybe," she finally said.

"Your tone means no."

"Lemme sleep on it, okay? Let's both sleep on it."

Paul mumbled something incoherent. Minutes later he was breathing heavily, with little chest-heaving shudders at first, then with breaths evening out to a steady rhythm.

Liddy lay, staring at the glowing red digits on her clock.

In the past two hours she'd gone from fury to self-doubting to holding Paul and comforting. How had that happened?

Something she'd cried out to him came back: *Even if you suspected Carl you'd cover for him, wouldn't you?*

But he'd deflected that, just like last night: *It's you that's crazy, go to Minton, don't believe that about Carl...don't damage...don't, don't, don't.*

She tossed and thrashed, feeling manipulated, feeling her anger roaring back...

35.

Sleep wouldn't come.

She lay for hours, her inner world hot and racing, trying to make sense out of too much that collided. The accident she couldn't remember (*why?*), the young blonde's face as it appeared that day on the glass (*and did look like Sasha Perry!*), and then oh God that scrawl for help she'd seen just nine hours ago in the shower. Now, at three in the morning, was her first chance to re-think *that* one. She'd pushed it down when it happened. Had to rush to get ready anyway, had welcomed the busyness that helped her block it…only now it came howling back in the way of all bogeymen who just lie in wait - then pounce in the darkest, most vulnerable hours. Liddy tossed and punched her pillow. The unlocked front door tormented her too - even more than again seeing Sasha and trying to chase her. Liddy was sure she had locked that damned door; could remember the rasping sound of the key as she turned it. But it was unlocked when they came back! Again and again, before her hand holding her outstretched key, she saw the door pop open and then, like a horror movie, creak open further into shadows. She remembered Paul's sharp intake of breath; could now, lying in darkness, imagine him thinking, *That's it, she's looney tunes. This whole damned move was futile and everything's gone to hell…*

Liddy rolled over, feeling her wild thoughts start to slow, give way to just a weary craving for peace. She even tried to rational-ize - hell, why not? Rationalizing made you feel better, it was probably what helped most people stay sane.

Maybe three a.m. is even a good time in disguise, she told

herself. A time to think through awfulness and deal with it in a way that busy daytime doesn't allow. Yeah, that's it, she thought. Three in the morning might really be the best self-shrink time - kind of like a mental/emotional purification plant.

She was dimly aware of a muffled *thud*, somewhere just outside that last thought she'd had. Startled, she peered across the room to the doorway, a tall, silent rectangle of lighter dark. No one was lurching through it, though; just her crazy imagination again. Gotta do something about that…try try try to get better…

She rolled back on the pillow, resuming her trip down Rationalize Lane. Admit it, she thought…returning from the restaurant she'd been semi-drunk and *wanting* to be angry. Paul had been vehement about Carl, pointing out that after all Liddy *had seen Sasha, hadn't she?* So maybe the lost, mysterious girl was alive and hiding *(from what?)* – but anyway there it was, re-thought and re-packaged - and oh how tempting it would be to believe that and end this self-torment, even if it did involve a lot of mea culpa. Somehow, Liddy thought, Sasha just appeared in my sketchbook and I built her up into some horror show-

But wait - if Sasha was indeed alive, why had Paul been so frantic about any connection between her and Carl?

Just nervousness, probably, from a hard working researcher whose grant had already been revoked once because of the recession, and who would naturally cringe from any association with a police-case missing person who had been in the news amid sad, awful coverage.

Liddy let out a pent-up breath. There, it was done. She'd pulled off the great gymnastic flip from fear and anger to re-thinking and accepting her own role in the craziness. A slow whisper escaped her lips. "Sasha Perry, I know you're alive because I saw you. Which means that the rest is nothing, just my overburdened mind playing tricks-"

Thud!

She heard it again, and this time it was louder, along with something like a long, soft sigh that came from the living room.

Liddy sat up. Was there a draft? Had she closed her studio window? She could only remember having opened it to let out the turp fumes. She turned to Paul who was sleeping, breathing heavily and exhausted. Uh, how would it go, after their unhappy night and his fears for her sanity, if she woke him and said, *I just heard something go bump?*

She got out of bed. Crept to the hall where she stopped, just outside the open door of her studio, and felt for an air current. Nothing. No draft at all; quiet in there.

A few more steps brought her to the living room, all darkened shapes dimly lit by a thin wash of moonlight. Carefully, her feet moved from hardwood floor to a rug as she headed for the nearest lamp, listening for a draft, looking around.

Then she stopped.

At first the shape seemed like a shaft of moonlight hitting one of the white cast iron columns. But it was too wide…and it was moving…swinging every so slightly, back and forth.

Liddy stared; felt her heart explode.

She sank to her knees, her eyes wide, frozen in terror as she stared at the face, chin down to its chest, neck broken by the cruel, taut rope, blond hair spilling down.

Breath was gone. She could not scream. Could not hear for the wild drumming of her pulse in her ears. A faint, mewling cry finally made its escape from her lips, and then another cry, louder this time, and then louder-

"Liddy."

Something crashed, and suddenly Paul was holding her. They were both on the floor with him holding her, frantic, asking what happened and watch out a lamp broke and my God, what happened, what happened. She tried to tell him, tried to point, up, up to the support beam that wasn't there anymore, the beam where Charlie Bass had hung himself and from which Sasha Perry now hung.

"It's her," she managed. "It's her."

She felt him shaking too, craning to where she was pointing.

"There's nothing there," he whispered frantically. "It's nothing, Lids...just...moonlight." He held her tighter. "My God, what happened?"

"I dreamt...there was a draft. Got up to see...found...her."

He was gone for seconds, got a different lamp on, then was back and holding her again, trembling, emitting words that fell over each other. "See? There's nothing. You were sleepwalking..."

She must have blacked out, then opened her eyes again back in bed with her nightgown soaked, her body sheened with sweat. Paul was half holding her, half toweling her dry, trying to comfort. She felt a tear from his face and shut her eyes tight, struggling not to see Sasha hanging again, her head down, her blond hair tumbling past her cheek to her shoulders, her body twirling in the cold light.

Paul was babbling, saying oh Liddy you must have dreamt it...then he was gone for seconds again and back with a glass his shaking hand spilled.

"Take this." He gave her a pill, held her head as she drank, then took one himself with the water she didn't finish. He climbed back into bed, up on his elbow holding her, whispering and babbling, Don't go walking out there, broken glass, broken glass.

"I saw her," Liddy whimpered over the torrent of his words. "Sasha is dead and she's *here*. Maybe *she* left our door open..."

"It's just us, Lids."

"No, I really saw her."

The pills started to work. Paul fell to Liddy's side and stayed that way, with his head on his pillow clinging to her as the blurry warmth of the drug finally crept over them.

Liddy's cries eased. Paul, simmering down, tried to comfort with stories of once sleepwalking in summer camp, and being sure he'd seen a ghost too.

A long time passed, but eventually, they slept.

36.

Something mechanical blared, jolting Liddy from a fitful sleep where a huge underwater chasm was sucking her down into blackness. She squinted her eyes open then squeezed them shut fast; with a moan plowed back into her pillow.

The bed shook as Paul lurched to slam off his alarm. Sunlight glared in from the drapes they'd forgotten to close.

"Hell," he said thickly, falling back to his pillow, exhaling like a dying man. His hand, cold marble, moved to her hand, then to her chest still heaving from the dream.

"Lids…"

"I'll call Minton," she whispered with her eyes closed.

She felt him press his brow to her shoulder, then rolled to him, feeling her heart start a fast knocking as if she'd been running. "It felt so real," she said painfully. "I know this sounds crazy, but it's as if that girl is really dead and wanted me to know."

He exhaled in a long breath. "You were sleepwalking."

"It was horrible. There have been other things I haven't mentioned because…I've been afraid. I *hate* this, I have to snap out of it."

"You will, we'll get through it," he said, squeezing her hand. He rolled away, and with a groan got his feet out of bed and onto the floor. Sat with his back turned and his head down, shielding his eyes from the light.

Liddy lay, still seeing like a shot to the heart Sasha hanging from that rope, her head down, her body moving slowly, right to left. It had seemed so real! The light had been silver bright from the moon and she had seen it, was remembering it now, happening before her eyes.

She felt Paul look back to her.

"Lids, don't…"

"What?"

"Stare into space like that."

A hysterical little laugh bubbled up. "You mean like I'm seeing a ghost?" She gave another bitter laugh. "I *am*. She was wearing a blue shirt. It seemed so real."

Paul shook his head; said nothing.

"That's the second time I saw a blue shirt…the first was in a dream waking that Sunday morning, the day we saw the loft." Liddy inhaled. "The shirt drifted against my face, choking me."

"Call Minton."

"Yeah, he'll fix it."

Paul grimaced, then shuffled in to shower. Liddy closed her eyes, listening to the sound of the pounding water, seeing the dark, underwater chasm of her dream pull her down again.

She blinked it away. Took a long, deep breath and checked the time. It was 7:15.

Too early to call Minton? No. Shrinks got crazed hysterical calls at all hours that just went to voice mail. Liddy reached for her cell phone.

The good doctor's recording was a slooow, infuriating drone that could make anyone crazy who wasn't already.

"I am in conference at the moment." *Yeah, you're still in bed, ha.* "If your call is an emergency, I urge you to call 9-1-1. If your call is not an emergency, leave your name, your number, and a short message…"

Was it infuriating or hilariously funny to hear you'd be queued up with fifty other bridge jumpers? The message made Liddy crack a smile, which was a blessing. It snapped her out of herself.

She practically spat out her message. "I realize this is off-schedule, but could you see me sometime sooner than Tuesday? Like, today, possibly?"

156

She disconnected, struggled out of bed, pulled on her kimono and brushed her hair. *Life is tough. If you don't laugh it's tougher.* Joan Rivers said that. Oh she was God's gift, that woman, especially if you're terrified that you've really lost it, gone seriously off the deep end, hanging by your chewed finger nails. As for calling Kerri, what would she say? I saw Sasha running in the street - then I saw her hanging in our apartment that had been locked up tight?

Maybe save it for Minton.

Liddy trudged to the kitchen and force-marched herself into busyness: started the coffee, emptied the dishwasher, fast-cooked eggs and slid them into a pita pocket. Grab 'n Run healthy breakfast, yessir. She'd always done it for Paul; wasn't about to let little things like sleepwalking and seeing ghosts and encroaching insanity stop her from doing it now.

Her hands still shook, though, and her heart kept up its tight, painful thudding. On her way to the kitchen she'd avoided looking out at the "hanging place" - as her frightened mind now called it - where Charlie Bass had done it, and Sasha too in whatever God help me last night was.

The smell of coffee was a balm, though, and as she poured it into Paul's travel mug Liddy bucked up enough to glance shakily out the kitchen door. The "hanging place" was now a realtor's too-pretty picture, bathed in sunlight slanting through the arched windows, with no sign of...either of them. Charlie Bass's beam he'd used for his rope was gone, disappeared, plastered over. The column Sasha Perry had swung from just stood there, a white, cast iron exclamation point glowing in the loft's openness.

"Oh!"

Pain hit and Liddy looked down. Must have gone half back to needed sleep staring out because the coffee filling Paul's mug had spilled and burned her hand. "Dammit," she whimpered, rushing to the sink and pouring cold water on it. She leaned her elbows on the sink's edge, watched the water splash and go down, down into that dark hole like her dream's underwater cavern. The sink's dark drain triggered something, like a flash or a vision, something just barely below the surface that she realized, suddenly, was important to remember. She shook her head, wracked her brain, but it didn't come.

Paul came in and she turned off the water, quickly wiped her hands on a paper towel.

He looked surprised, buttoning his shirt, peering around at the kitchen humming.

"Cancel Minton," he said, lamely attempting humor, losing a bit of his haggard look at seeing his sports duffle with his healthy eats laid out next to it, everything lined up as usual on the counter.

The hand was stinging but Liddy gave him her bravest smile. He seemed to be having the reaction she'd hoped he'd have: *she's functioning, already better by the light of day.* He'd been pathetic last night during their argument - had actually...cried? Liddy saw again how beaten and defeated he'd seemed; remembered too the awful thought that had come to her: *just who here is crazy?*

Anybody, that's who. Horrendous pressure can undo anyone. Liddy was too tired to think; didn't know what to think; craved with all her being just one blessed day of normalcy, please.

She stepped closer to Paul, reached to push a lock of hair off his brow. "Everything's going to be okay," she said, trying to mean it. A day with him not falling apart would also help. *Just one blessed day of normalcy, please?*

He sat on the edge of a barstool, looking worried with his lips pressed thin. "You really think so?"

"Yes," she lied, feeling her chest tighten, dreading the day.

"Going to paint?"

"Yup, it's better therapy than Alex Minton." She started putting Paul's things into his duffel. "No choice anyway. I'm behind on a project, another watercolor." Then she stopped what she was doing, and looked back to him. "Painting saves me. It really does, a million times better than listening to Minton drone. It's like…I go off into colorful worlds and lose myself in them, and in the process I find myself. Does that make sense?"

He nodded wearily; gave a crooked smile. "Sounds like an artist."

At the front door he gave her a long hug. "Let's have a re-do on going out," he said. "Find some little French restaurant and hide, just us."

"What? No socializing?"

"God forbid."

She smiled a real smile this time. "I'd love that."

Another hug, and Paul left with hurried reminders to lock up. "The slide bolt *and* the keypad."

Liddy closed the door, then stared for a long moment at the knob. When Paul's steps receded down the stairwell, she opened the door again. Stepped out into the empty hall and bent, peering into the keyhole. "I did lock you last night," she said, very softly. "You know I did."

The keyhole stayed…just a keyhole, mute, revealing nothing.

She breathed in; straightened. Since last night - their tension, the unlocked door, the three a.m. brain gnashing - she'd wanted to have another look at that lock. For what? She didn't know.

Back inside she closed the door, flipped the bolt, punched in the security code, then turned back to the apartment.

The sun had moved, and with it the shadows. Light angling in from higher up now cast a shorter, squatter darkness behind the white column, and it *moved.* Clouds outside sailed in gusts before the sun, sending every shadow in the room into weird little dances.

Spray the plants?

Not yet. The days were cooling. No rush there.

Liddy raced, as fast as her bad leg could carry her, through the moving shadows to her studio.

37.

Four mason jars half full of water: one for each of the three primary colors – red, yellow, blue – and one for rinsing her brushes, her cherished, expensive sable brushes which were a whole different set from the ones she used for oil painting. As in the kitchen, Liddy force-marched herself, struggling to push down her galloping fears. *Denial? Who me?* Her hands still shook but she started to get excited, her preparations bringing her closer to her cherished other world that provided escape. Onto her palette she squeezed out gorgeous blobs from her Winsor & Newton watercolor tubes; then to the up-tilted surface of her draftsman's table she tacked her Strathmore watercolor paper – big sheets, eighteen by twenty-four inches. A foot away, on the table's flat arm to the side, she put a bowl of water and a sponge, and then, neatly, she stacked more sheets of Strathmore in case of mistakes. *In art you can cover mistakes, isn't that great? Just start afresh or lay on more pigment.*

She stopped, for seconds, taking deep breaths, looking out and around.

Watercolor meant no turpentine fumes, which meant that the window top could stay closed, thus giving Liddy a sense of being extra hermetically safe in her cocoon. She needed that today, needed it bad. Exhaling with something close to relief, she sat at her draftsman's table and spread her hands apart, gripping its corners as if to embrace it. Today she could sit instead of stand, just slouch way down with her nose close to the paper, her hand moving the brushes, dipping, spreading colors, watching the shapes and colors and her whole new world appear.

Let nothing intrude, please. Let nothing else enter my poor, aching head...

She started her first, preliminary sketch. Holding her mechanical pencil, her hand started to sweep and move, like a conductor's baton. The project called for a scary fantasy: delicate fairies trapped on a rocky crag fleeing a down-swooping, heavy-clawed griffin - a nasty beast with the body, tail and back legs of a lion, the fierce head, wings and talons of an eagle. Liddy's hand worked faster. She was in that world now, her swirling thin pencil lines starting to take forms that cowered, ran, struggled...

A buzz startled her. It took a second to realize what it was.

Her cell phone, sitting a foot from her hand.

"I'm quite swamped but can fit you in at five," Alex Minton droned in his flat tone. "Would you describe your situation as serious?"

She wanted to bray laughter. *Oh har, well I'm still alive if that's what you mean,* she wanted to say, but quelled it instead with, "That may be for you to determine." She squeezed her eyes tight, fighting being yanked out of her cloud.

"Describe briefly, please? To help assess your issue."

She squeezed her eyes tighter as her heart took off again. "I saw a ghost last night." It astounded her to hear herself say that. "In our living room. Hanging from a rope."

Silence at the other end. But not a long silence as human data banks scanned and searched.

"Have you had any thoughts of harming yourself?"

"No." Liddy opened her eyes; felt them sting and fill.

"That's good. It's very good." The voice became comforting. "You've been under great stress. The main cause as we've discussed would be your accident, traumatic in itself, plus your concussion which may have left emotional issues if not specific neural damage. Seeing or sensing some, uh, 'being' connects to feelings of desperation, and is more common than you might think."

161

"I didn't *sense* a being, I *saw* it, maybe sleepwalking but it sure *seemed* real." Liddy gripped her phone hard as a tear spilled down her cheek. "A blond female ghost, hanging by the neck."

Another silence, a brief one. "Then we must discuss the significance of hallucinations, perhaps schedule you for another look at the possibility of neurological damage. I've reviewed your case history and don't believe that to be the case, however. Mainly, I think we should return to the source of your issue. The accident, and why it happened."

"I don't *know*." Liddy hunched forward. "I've *told* you and *told* you, I just don't remember - what good has going on and on about 'returning to the source' done?" She swiped furiously at another tear. Minton was droning, something else about hallucinations but she wasn't hearing; was squeezing her eyes shut with her shoulders bunched and one hand holding an imaginary rope to the other side of her head ready to join Charlie and Sasha until, thank God, the droning stopped and she could finally say Yes, agreeing to the five o'clock appointment.

Then she hung up. Stared at her drawing with her eyes streaming.

Well that spoiled it. She'd found a whole half hour's peace, the shrink had made her crazy again, and the colors in her mind were gone. Thin, dead pencil lines faced her, just empty souls on paper, stillborn.

She picked up her pencil, at least. It belonged there, in her hand squeezing it *tight tight tight* to hold down her sense of helplessness, the bigger gale of tears that threatened. Then she saw a small face peer up at her, feeling the same, feeling just as terrified with round eyes that begged, wings that struggled to open and flee. So she gulped air and dove into the paper again, rescuing that little fairy, and then another and then another, nearly forgetting her thudding heart as the hours flew and her pencil flew, filling out wings and the delicate lift of arms as each delicate being fled the griffin nearly upon them with claws splayed viciously.

Quick. Colors.

With a jerky motion she grabbed the sponge. Dipped it in water, squeezed it but not too much, then ran it across the drawing for the blurred effect of adding watercolor to moist paper. She was excited again. No, she was in a frenzy, desperate to get this painting right – highly emotional like what she was feeling, so she reached down to the side of the table for the wheel and raised the drawing; tilted it *up* so it was nearly vertical.

Perched now on her tall stool, she went to work with bigger brushes first, diving into colors and mixing, applying the first gauzy layer that sank in fast, absorbed to make a brightly violent, orange-pink background. Sunrise or sunset? *Either.* Liddy's hands guided themselves. Small brushes flew next, swished in water, mixed colors, added layers of burnt orange, gold ochre, light brown and pale charcoal for the crag the fairies had to escape...work from light to dark, always in watercolors... Faces terrified and terrorizing came to life; brushes heavy with watered crimson and cadmium and cobalt violet smeared on and dripped brightly. Liddy caught the drips and brushed them into wind and the griffin's snorting and then crashing lightning in raw sienna – oh...

Oh...

She stepped back.

Raw sienna, not so good for the lightning, and she'd mixed the brush into too much water and the sienna was dripping into the crimson, the colors mixing and dripping down into the white and rose she'd mixed for clouds and...

Liddy took another step back.

From the bright wetness a face was emerging. Long hair in the cadmium yellow mixed for the lightning. White, rose and peach blending into woeful eyes that wept and begged.

Breath stopped. Liddy's heart stopped too as words emerged and dripped beneath the face.

Help me, said the words.

Her hands went to her cheeks as she saw them, clearly. No doubting this, not sleepwalking…the face and those words were there, dripping. Liddy's heart slammed as she stood, transfixed, imprisoned by those colors that dripped and coalesced, changed but still…still there, the words and the face. The eyes sagging now, looking straight at her, begging, begging.

"What can I do?" Liddy whimpered, barely hearing herself over the drumming in her ears. "What can I do?" she cried, feeling her whole soul wrenched out of her.

The grieving face floated, as if in permanent, begging limbo, resisting the pull of other too-wet colors sliding down.

The words stayed too: *Help me.*

In a whoosh, Liddy felt all breath rush out of her. She bent slightly, clutching her belly, and burst into tears.

Somehow made it back to her phone on the table. Managed to hit her speed dial.

38.

Beth was there in minutes. Maybe more. Liddy must have gotten the front door open and passed out. Came to stretched on the couch with a worried Beth on the ottoman leaning to her, squeezing her hand, patting her arm with her other hand.

"I don't believe that," Beth was saying, her voice coming from a blurred far away.

"What?" Liddy whispered, aware that she'd been speaking, or trying to.

"You just said you'd finally and officially had a psychotic break. People who've really flipped out don't talk like that." Beth's face was distraught, her hand was clammy. "Tell me again," she said gently. "What happened?"

The ceiling swam. The light-headedness was easing a little. "...in the studio. Sasha's face...in the watercolor. She wrote...*help me.*"

"Hang tight."

Beth went. Stared, for what seemed endless, frightening moments at the wild, swooping colors, the histrionic figures...and the mournful face, the begging words beneath it. "Oh God," she whispered, very softly. "Oh God, oh God," she nearly cried, her hand to her mouth as she hurried back, stopping in the kitchen for water.

"Drink, your lips are dry," she said, handing Liddy the glass, pulling the ottoman closer. Liddy sipped and coughed a little. Beth got more upset, so Liddy forced her legs made of cement off the couch and onto the floor; insisted on sitting but with her head in her hands.

"You saw?"

"Yes."

Liddy raised her eyes. Saw Beth's alarm.

"You're thinking maybe I did it? Went crazy, painted the face myself and those words?"

Beth swallowed, then shook her head. Her eyes were deadly serious. "I've never known you to talk of ghosts or see things or...hell, *none* of it has ever been you - but this is worse than the nightmares. What's happened? *Something* new has happened."

Liddy dropped her head; poured out last night in long, shaky breaths. Seeing or thinking she'd seen Sasha Perry running from her. Then the unlocked front door that should have been locked; then, three in the morning, Sasha's ghost hanging over there. Liddy raised a finger to point. Now...Sasha's face in the watercolor, begging for help...

Liddy's face crumpled, tried not to cry. "So if you like ghost stories or believe in that stuff, she must really be dead, and she's come to tell me and wants help, revenge. Isn't that how ghost stories go?"

Beth stared at her. *If you like ghost stories or believe in that stuff...* It sounded totally, undeniably sane. There'd been almost a note of self-deprecating humor: *Isn't that how ghost stories go?* She tried to process it all. "Dare I ask what Paul's reaction was to the ghost?"

A whisper: "Double hysteria but supportive." Liddy inhaled slowly, deeply. "We'd had an argument before it, about Carl. We were with him at a restaurant-"

"Wait. You're so pale. Have you eaten?"

"Couldn't. Coffee this morning..."

"Oh my Lord, great. Fainting on an empty stomach."

Beth got Liddy to the kitchen, where she drooped on a barstool while Beth microwaved oatmeal mixed with milk and lots of sugar. "For strength," she said, stirring the mush, pushing the bowl to Liddy. "My mother used to swear by sugary oatmeal. You can *have* your shrinks, oatmeal *cures*."

A spoonful of it stopped near Liddy's mouth. "Shrink. Oh jeez, what time is it?"

"Four-forty."

A minute later Beth was on her phone to Minton, saying she was a friend and that, so sorry, Liddy would have to cancel.

"Yes, she's okay. Has to rest, that's all. Thank you, I'll tell her." Disconnecting, Beth announced that the good doctor was behind anyway. "Lots of emergencies," she said, rolling her eyes. "Freaking out in his waiting room is *not* where you'd want to be."

Liddy managed the weakest little snicker as she spooned more oatmeal, commenting that it really did make you feel better. It also felt better just to talk, spew everything to a loving friend without fear of being called crazy.

Beth leaned and put her elbows on the counter, facing her. "So...a fight about Carl?"

Liddy filled her in. The evening at Righetti's. Carl's date pushing the sketch of Sasha at him, insisting he'd known her because she'd been in his class. "You should have seen him practically ducking the sketch, refusing to look at it."

"Ah - and *why* would he squirm and refuse to look if it were just another student?"

"Exactly. He's usually smoother; could have said, 'pretty, nope, never saw her' - only he'd been drinking." Liddy frowned. "Which again isn't like Carl. He hates loss of control from too much booze, and he'd been planning to return to the lab for serious work."

"Drinking makes it sound like he was nervous. Deteriorating, even."

A nod. "There's been tension. He was mad at Paul because the cops tried to pursue a Sasha connection to him and got nowhere."

"Wait - Carl was mad at *Paul*?"

"And me." Liddy toyed mournfully with her spoon. Her

strength was returning. "Carl had seen my sketch of Sasha, blamed me for the cops' visit because…I'm guessing…Paul must have mentioned or complained that I'd gone to them. That seems the only logical explanation."

Beth frowned. "So they'd been talking about this. The case."

"Apparently."

"Why? Sounds like mutual nervousness."

Liddy sighed; tapped her spoon on the edge of her empty bowl. It made a sad, hollow sound in the kitchen. "After last night's fight, I realized Paul would cover for Carl even if he did suspect something. Either denial or twin ambition, it amounts to the same." She sighed again. "Anyway, slippery Carl told the cops he'd never laid eyes on Sasha, showed there was no record of her in his class…then last night - boom! His drunk date insisted she'd just heard that Sasha only *audited* his course, that's why no record. Things got really tense after that."

"Tell the police." Beth started angrily fussing with the pepper shaker.

"I'd wanted to. Paul read my thoughts and got frantic, insisted I was being paranoid. How could Sasha be harmed by *anyone* if I saw her running in the street? Why damage the world-shaking important work they were doing?" Liddy shook her head. "I really would have called Kerri Blasco this morning if I hadn't seen - correction, sleepwalked and seen - Sasha swinging from a rope in our living room. So that confirms my paranoia, right?"

"Bullshit." Beth's cell phone buzzed. She slammed the pepper shaker down and checked her screen; ignored it; muttered about letting it go to voice mail.

"A client?"

"Just some annoying hedge funder confirming a five-thirty." She pocketed her phone and started pacing angrily. "If you call the cops you'll be Anonymous. No one needs to know where it came from."

"Yes they will. Right after my hearing it last night?" Liddy took an unhappy breath and looked out the window. It had clouded over; was an early dusk with the air looking almost dark. "Last night's argument...Paul actually cried, insisted any connection between Carl and Sasha was off the wall craziness, told me don't don't don't."

"Sure, even a whiff of this would threaten their whole grant, right?"

"You know how the media would jump on it - that's *their* nightmare, every story outdoing the competition in salaciousness." Liddy's brow furrowed. "What kills me is, Paul's just as brilliant as Carl and could carry on alone – maybe not get the thing done in time - but they're way past the halfway point; have shown that they've really got something there, and Big Pharma's excited. Aren't they bottom line guys anyway, these corporations? If they smell a profit, do they *care* if half the team gets embroiled in a scandal?"

"Maybe they do."

"That's what Paul thinks." Liddy shook her head. "I don't understand why he feels so beholden, why he clings to his cherished idea that he and Carl have been such friends for decades. Carl's just used him – at points in his life where it suited him."

"Paul doesn't want to see it, who can argue with denial – who *cares*?" Beth stopped pacing, drew together all her concern and outrage, and, pointing back over her shoulder to the studio, said, "That face in the painting is the worst, Lids." She wheeled her arm around and pointed toward the front. "Ditto me finding you sprawled in a dead faint in the open doorway. This thing hurting you has gotten way more serious than the nightmares. You gotta take action. Didn't we talk about saving yourself?"

Liddy was blinking; staring at nothing, looking startled, almost. "It just hit," she breathed slowly, "that I've had the feeling all along, deep down, that Carl was somehow involved with Sasha -

and my nightmares, all of it." She searched Beth's eyes, almost excited. "The feeling's been there since *before* last night - it just hit," she repeated.

"Oh Lids, your memory's returning."

"Did I mention I took Carl's date's number? She said she knew the person who saw Sasha in Carl's class, and would vouch for it."

"This gets better and better."

"They'll still know the tip-off came from me. Think this will lead to divorce?"

"No." Beth looked around. "Where's your phone?"

39.

They looked in the front where Liddy fainted, then through the living room and finally found it under a chair. The time was 5:05. Liddy took the couch again and Beth hunched on the ottoman, watching her turn up the sound and call Kerri Blasco.

"Liddy, hello!" Kerri's voice was welcoming. It sounded as if she was in a street somewhere, moving fast. Traffic blared and other cop voices sounded, blunt and hurried.

Liddy told her. "Carl Finn's date, Nicki something. Claims to know someone who remembers Sasha auditing Carl Finn's class. Auditing leaves no record. Here's Nicki's number." She dictated it.

"This is huge, big thanks," Kerri told her over the shout of someone clamoring for EMTs. Then, in spite of what was going on at her end Kerri said, "How *are* you, Liddy? How are you feeling?"

A quick glance traded with Beth, and Liddy said, "Horrible. Seeing ghosts. Definitely losing my mind."

Not a beat missed at the other end. "I'm near," Kerri said. "Would you like me to come over?"

Beth was waving her arms and nodding furiously, but Liddy hesitated. "Yes, but I don't want my husband to know."

Just the thing to catch a cop's attention. Beth almost smirked at the slip. Her own phone rang and she rose and walked away, answering.

"What time does he get home?" Kerri asked.

"Late. He usually works late. I don't know why I said that."

"No worries, I look like anyone anyway. I'll give this Nicki's number to my partner and be there in five minutes, sound good?"

In that moment, a weight like a boulder lifted from Liddy's chest. Having Beth there was comfort; having Kerri Blasco coming felt – hopefully not irrationally – like being rescued.

"Sounds very good," Liddy said. "Yes, please come."

She disconnected to the sound of Beth arguing on her phone. "Yes, I *know* when the Asian markets open. Sorry, I've been delayed, I'll be there ASAP."

Liddy felt bad.

"I've made you late," she said when Beth hung up.

"Tough, this guy's a jerk. I've got the exclusive and he'll just damn wait." Beth was pacing near Charlie's plants, stopping to finger some leaves, then touch the telescope. She took a quick look through it, lost interest and turned. "Besides, I'd like to meet this Kerri Blasco. She sounds amazing."

"She is."

Beth glanced back to the foliage. "Been spraying 'em?"

"Yup, no apparitions." Liddy came to stand with her friend while they waited. They stared down at the darkening street, busy with people heading for home and the bars. Liddy sighed, "Something else happened - before last night at the restaurant I saw the same mournful girl's face in the shower stall, in the steam on the glass. The mist turned into her tears."

Beth turned to her, strained. "Jesus, Lids. You didn't say."

"Brains fried. Still recovering from the watercolor."

The front bell sounded, and they opened to smiling Kerri Blasco in black cargo pants and a black, low-scooped T-shirt under a gray blazer. Shoulder-length dark blond hair fell to her shoulders.

Her grip was strong, and she cracked a joke about just seeing a man and his poodle with matching pink-dyed hair. "I swear that dog's fur was blow-dried." Her laugh was infectious, confident, and after introductions and taking a seat on the couch and punching something *ping ping ping* into her phone, she crossed her legs and got down to it. Her gun was clearly visible in her ankle holster.

"That Nicki? Grade A intel," she told Liddy, noting the deep, sleep-deprived shadows under her eyes. "And surprise - ESP or something, because minutes after you called, Nicki did too, drunk and crying. She'd probably spent the whole day working up to it, is mad at her now ex who she says dumped her after a fight, so she spewed the same thing you said about Sasha. Gave us a name to contact."

Liddy's lips parted. The detective smiled and read her thoughts. "Nicki will probably even taunt Carl Finn about what she did. In any case, there'll be no one guessing this came from you."

"Relief," Liddy said faintly, beyond excited. "He's my husband's partner."

"I know. Relax, you're out of the loop." Kerri got out her notebook.

Liddy quickly described Carl in the restaurant: his unusual drinking, refusal to look at the Sasha sketch, tension when his date tried to push it at him. Kerri scribbled. Liddy next described Paul's upset two nights ago over Kerri's surprise visit to Carl – "...sounded like you really shook him and he took it out on Paul." Just then Beth's phone rang. She checked it, muttered "jerk again," and got up to answer.

Curiously, Kerri stopped taking notes to listen as Beth told the caller, "Yes, *yes,* I'm on my way. The traffic's terrible."

Then she stepped back to the couch to pick up her purse and a tote full of manila folders. Some of the folders had slid out. Kerri nodded approvingly. "Very good. You lie like a cop."

"Real estate." Beth made a face, suddenly hurried and pushing the folders back in. "They give special classes in lying. Okay, I gotta go. Will you be needing my number?" she asked Kerri.

The detective held up her phone. "Already have it. 'Find your dream home with BethanyHarms.com, real estate professional,'" she said from memory, then read off digits. "That your private cell number?"

"Yes." Beth looked too hurried to be surprised. "Call if anything. No, sit, Lids, I'll let myself out." She shook again with Kerri, moved to go, then at the door turned back to Liddy. "Tell everything, Lids. Including that couple fighting across the street."

She set the slide bolt to snap shut behind her, and left.

Liddy stared at the door after it closed. Kerri studied her features; watched her confused gaze move from the door to one of the arched windows fronting a small forest and a high-powered telescope.

"That's odd," Liddy said. "I don't remember telling Beth that."

"What?"

It seemed so long ago; now it came rushing back.

"When we first moved in, Paul started to spend a lot of time staring through that telescope. I'm not sure if it bothered me, but soon after I couldn't sleep, and went to look through it around two in the morning, and saw a couple fighting. First they were having wild, crazy sex, then half an hour later they were arguing furiously."

Kerri frowned, nodded.

"He hit her, hit her bad. I told Paul the next morning and he said it wasn't our business."

"Shut you down, huh?"

"He just said couples fight, happens all the time. He was rushing to work. I should have…God, what could I have done?" Liddy hated how lame that sounded; looked guiltily toward the telescope. "The girl was blond. Looked for a second like that sketch I'd made of Sasha, I wasn't sure."

Kerri was on her feet. "Show me which apartment?"

Liddy did. Adjusted the telescope, looked through it, found the fighting couple's window and stepped back. "The shade's been pulled since that night," she said as Kerri fiddled with the eyepiece and looked in. Liddy watched her, then peered left down the street; breathed in, plunged. "Yesterday evening I saw or thought I saw the same girl. Her face was bruised and up close I was sure she was Sasha Perry - she even wore a Winnie the Pooh stud in her right ear. I called to her, and she ran."

Kerri looked at Liddy as if she hadn't heard right. The features she saw were clearly embarrassed, unsure.

"Where was this?" Kerri said evenly, going back to the 'scope, squinting into it.

"On Mercer, heading south toward me. Actually brushed my shoulder as she passed – which is when I called to her, said her name out loud. She got scared, ran back to Prince and disappeared in the crowd in front of that building you're looking at."

Kerry straightened; scribbled in her notebook. Liddy turned from her, sent her gaze back across the long room to the closed front door.

"It's the damnedest thing," she said almost painfully, sounding as if she were talking to herself. "I have no memory of telling Beth about that fighting couple. How could she know?"

Again Kerri looked at her, eyebrows raised, her silence prodding.

Liddy threw up both hands. "Well, my memory's been in the crapper. It'll probably come back at some odd moment, like all the rest of the horrible stuff that's been happening."

"Like what? Tell me from the beginning. Your sketch of Sasha."

"You'll call the men in the white coats."

"No way. From the beginning, please. If you've already told me, tell me again. Show me."

Out came the plastic bottle to spray the plants. Liddy showed how the mist formed – only now it was just mist against a darkening sky, not the weeping, begging young woman's face of that first apparition. "Imagination, right? Cruel tricks of a

175

damaged mind?" she said, leading the way to the bathroom and the shower stall, describing how the same tearful, begging face had appeared on the steamed-up glass. "That was half an hour before I saw, or thought I saw, Sasha running from me."

Liddy leaned back out to the living room and pointed. "Then she appeared to me last night at three in the morning, hanging dead from that column. I screamed. Paul came running and said nothing was there. I guess I was sleepwalking. That's why I didn't call you. I woke up convinced I'd really lost my mind."

40.

Oh boy.

Kerri remembered Hank Kubic going on about Shakespeare and Dostoyevsky and Macbeth and Lady Macbeth. *Ask her if she's been sleepwalking. Seeing dead people.*

She stepped out of the bathroom and stared at the white, cast iron column. The light outside had grown darker. She asked, "Your husband was sleeping when you saw this?"

"Yes." Liddy eased past her, went around turning on lamps. "And the place was locked tight with the security system on. Paul always checks."

Kerri got out her phone and approached the column. To Liddy's surprise she photographed it from all angles, high, low, and then the ceiling. It was white smoothness up there. "Did you notice what the rope was hanging from?" she asked, looking up. Most of the cases in Hank's report were very specific describing their hallucinations, down to the merest invisible detail.

Liddy came; pointed to where Charlie Bass's hanging beam was now plastered over, and shrugged. "So she was hanging from nothing, a beam that isn't there anymore. See? Time to call the funny farm."

Kerri had made a mental list of Liddy's responses. *Imagination, right? Cruel tricks of a damaged mind. I saw, or thought I saw Sasha. Time to call the funny farm, the men in white coats. I woke up convinced I'd lost my mind.*

Then Hank Kubic waving his steak knife flashed. "'Is this a dagger I see before me?' Poor Mac really thought he saw it! Both he and his missus saw terror that wasn't there and couldn't be persuaded otherwise."

Kerri thought while she moved and took pictures; asked questions whose answers seemed to follow the same pattern.

Liddy made sad jokes about her state. She was just beaten down, there was no aggression or defensiveness to her. Kerri had plowed through Hank's case files and more similar stuff. Lots of clinical gibberish but she did see the big picture...and still listened to her gut. She was kneeling at the base of the white column, holding her phone and looking up, when something occurred. "How did you know where Charlie's hanging beam was?"

"Saw it," Liddy said, watching her. "When Beth first showed us the loft."

"Oh right, she was your agent?"

"Yes."

"When did you first see the apartment?"

"August ninth. It was a Sunday."

That prompted a smile as Kerri rose. "See that? Nothing wrong with your memory." She turned back to peer at the line of tall plants. "That window faces south. The summer sun must have really fried those greens. Who took care of them before you came along?"

"Beth did, every day. She said they made the place look nicer, especially since Charlie left the rest such a mess."

Kerri's eyes were quick; she'd heard hardened, experienced cops say there was so much *behind* them, recording, connecting, moving like benign lasers around the toughest crime scenes. Now she scanned again, from the window to the white column, then back toward the bathroom.

"The shower stall mist. Did you see the face in there again? A second time?"

"No. Just one sold-out appearance."

"Were you able to make it go away or did it stay?"

"I wiped it away." Liddy gave a shudder. "It stayed gone, but now seems to have moved to my studio – the face just appeared *in a painting*. When you see it, you'll really want to call the booby hatch."

Kerri shook her head. "No, show me."

Lady Macbeth and nearly every case in Hank's file were defensive and irrationally vain, always seeing themselves as victims - never sad sacks attempting humor, poking fun at themselves suggesting you call the funny farm. In fact, without exception they were devoid of humor.

"This isn't a waste of police time?" Liddy asked as they crossed the living room. "Spending time with a crazy person who sees ghosts?"

"You're not crazy," Kerri said. "Let's see that painting."

41.

The eyes were heartbreaking, and the young woman's lips were parted in anguish, as if crying out the words *Help me* still dripping beneath. Liddy herself was surprised at how lurid she'd made the colors, the hysterical flailing of figures terrified and terrorizing in mortal struggle. Kerri, after staring at the painting for long moments, commented on that: hysterical or not, the work was a clear depiction of good battling evil.

"I must have been in a trance," Liddy said, slumped on the window seat clutching a throw pillow.

Kerry looked at her. "Subconscious art is the most honest." She went back to the painting and frowned. *Odd*: much of it was still wet, colors had slid, but the tearful, begging face and the cry for help beneath it stayed suspended. From the letter p in *Help* a drop of red had slid down and become a small ruby, hanging, growing.

Whew. This was something.

Kerri took Liddy's chair at her draftsman's table; studied the drooping figure across from her. "Have you ever believed in ghosts? Like, as a kid?"

"No." Faint head shake. "Used to laugh at Scooby Doo and his ghosts."

"That's a cartoon."

"That's where ghosts belong. In cartoons. Scare novels."

"Ever read *Turn of the Screw*?"

"Tried to. Found the text turgid. Started the movie and stopped it."

"Why?"

"Depressing. You know the governess is doomed."

So she'd liked cartoons as a kid, never believed in ghosts, and avoided depressing stories. This was not a person prone to hysteria or wild, unhappy subjects. Kerri tapped her index finger thoughtfully on the drawing table, then asked, "You paint thriller book covers mostly?"

Nod.

"Why is that?"

An indifferent shrug. "That's where there's the most demand. I started out doing romance covers and a few non-fiction covers, then did one thriller and the publisher went ape, spread the word and I found myself in demand."

So she'd backed into the thriller thing, hadn't sought it out. Kerri glanced up to the window behind Liddy. The upper sash was open a little but the alarm was on.

She asked about that.

"Oh." Liddy turned to look up, then with a groan climbed onto the window seat, pushed the top sash closed and locked it. "The top part isn't connected to the alarm," she said, scrunching back down to her pillow on the window seat. "I paint with oils, too, and turpentine fumes are toxic, so we just had the bottom sash wired to let the top open, let out the fumes."

She glanced at the wires and small bits of hardware stretched across the sill behind her. "But alarms can't keep out ghosts, can they?" she grimaced, looking back with a shudder. "I've become afraid to fall asleep. Just looking at the bed makes me spaz and think, nooo, what's tonight going to bring?"

Kerri's eyes were sympathetic. She nodded and said, very quietly, "I've been there."

Liddy raised surprised eyes to her. "You? You seem so strong."

"No one's that strong." Kerri inhaled. "I've gone what felt like months without sleep, seeing a shrink who didn't help, stumbling through days. I just had to muddle through it." She saw Liddy's eyes open wider, so she shrugged; continued.

"One night two years ago I found myself on a roof with a perp's gun in my face, his finger starting to pull the trigger. I knew I was dead." A hesitation; the words speeded up. "The SOB had to make it even more terrifying by pressing his knee on my chest, pushing his barrel to my head screaming how he couldn't wait to see my brains splatter all over…and then" – she gestured – "*bang*, there was a shot and blood and brains did splatter - only not mine, my partner Alex saved me, shot the slime who *fell on me*, bleeding, his face all exploded, his brain squish running down my neck."

Liddy was gaping at her and she stopped. "Hell, I upset you. Last thing I want to do."

"No… My God, how did you survive? Is it crazy to say your story helps?"

Kerri gestured; smiled. "Not at all. I've often thought people going through misery and seeing shrinks should just get together in the shrinks' waiting rooms and trade stories. It would help more."

"*Yes*, because you don't feel so alone." Liddy thought, and her brow furrowed. "So…what happened after that? You said you went months…"

Kerri glanced up to the mournful face begging for help; pressed her lips tight for a moment.

"Nightmares so vivid I'd wake up screaming and scrabbling to wipe the creep's brains off my neck, or gasping for breath because his knee was still pressing my chest. That was the first time I'd actually seen someone die. In homicide, you arrive *after* they've been killed, they're just…bodies lying there, no threat to anyone, surrounded by other cops who got there first, they're all neatly cordoned off by our yellow crime scene tape - but that night…he just jumped out at me." Kerri shook her head slowly. "It didn't help that I'd just had a miscarriage and was going through a divorce at the time, that I'd been a weeping wreck *before* that night. Bad things like to happen in bunches, don't they? I still get nightmares, though way less often. Isn't that great? A stunning improvement?"

"I'm so sorry..." Liddy was amazed to find herself forgetting herself, coming out of herself and liking this woman - a lot. "God, what you went through, so awful..."

"No one escapes," Kerri said gravely. "I've seen every kind of person in places high and low, and I've come to that conclusion. Everyone at some time goes through some long nightmare. Parents broken-hearted over their kids, best friends turning out to be not friends at all, wives discovering their husbands aren't who they thought they were – or the other way around. You just have to hang on, let the scars form."

Liddy was nodding, slowly, and Kerri added: "Those nightmares I had? They were *really vivid*, seemed totally real and in the first minutes of waking up I'd still be shaking, convinced they *were* real. Does it help to know that?"

Liddy met her eyes; inhaled hugely and smiled. "Oh yes. If someone like you can go through something like that and come out in one piece..."

"I did." Kerri gave a little laugh. "I'm as sane as anyone now, which may not be saying a whole lot." She got to her feet, brushed invisible lint off her black pants, then looked back at the painting.

Her mouth opened. "Is it my imagination or has her weeping face gotten bigger?"

Liddy rose too. "Gotten bigger. Drooping longer 'cause the paint's still wet."

Kerri noted the sane, quiet interpretation, but for a little comic relief faked a scared look. "Are hallucinations catching?"

"Yeah, that must be it."

42.

They went to the kitchen, where the sharp-eyed detective moved around, looking here, there, stopping before a venerable old photo of a sailboat: into a tarnished plaque screwed into the old frame was the name *Seafarer.* "That your boat?" she asked.

"Was. It looks like Carl Finn and another friend are going to buy it."

"Oh?"

Kerri's raised eyebrows prodded. Liddy pointed to a different photo: Paul, Carl and Ben Allen before the docked boat, with Finn planted boisterously in front of other two, hamming it up and hoisting beer cases. "Carl and this other guy," she said, naming Allen.

The same photo Kerri took in Ben Allen's office, and had in her phone. She nodded to him. "Is he a friend too?"

"Of mine? Hardly. Actually, not really so much of Paul's either, as far as I can see. Ben and Carl have been pals since med school. 'Partners in crime,' Ben likes to say, and keeps saying, thinks that's uproarious. He met Paul through Carl three years ago. They all love sailing, that's their glue."

Liddy frowned suddenly. Stared harder at the photo, specifically at Ben Allen. "My head's still whirling from the painting but…wasn't Ben questioned months ago when Sasha was arrested for…" She stopped; looked confused.

"Forging his narcotics prescription," Kerri supplied. "Ben Allen insisted he knew nothing of what she did. It seems to have ended there." *But not really*, Kerri thought, her mind as always pursuing a line leading from Allen to Carl Finn. She wanted to know more about Finn.

Liddy still stared at Allen, looking almost pathetic with her head tilted as if trying to remember more. "I read about that recently, when the news started talking about the case again," she said foggily. "Remembered the other night, now...can't."

Kerri diverted her, moving around to other framed photos: the same three men with the sun on their faces trimming the jib, tacking and coming about, laughing it up in the stern waving their beer bottles. Lots of photos with Paul and the guys. Over the counter there was a single photo: Paul and Liddy embracing, hanging on to rigging.

Kerri stepped closer, studying the picture. "Just one of you and Paul?" she asked.

Liddy gave a shrug. "I have others, just haven't hung them yet." Which meant she didn't like them.

Kerri pointed back to the photo whose copy was in her cell phone. "Did you take that one?"

"Yes, but I didn't go out with them." Liddy turned away, got busy with the pepper shaker Beth had fiddled with. Kerri said nothing, so Liddy told the pepper shaker, "I'd been arguing with Paul. We'd planned to go out alone, a romantic day, and then the Boys Club called and invited themselves and Paul said Sure! Just like that. Like he hadn't promised."

Kerri frowned to herself. Was this the first glimpse of...something new? "Boy, I'd be jealous," she said. "Or feel understandably hurt."

Liddy shook her head, turned back to the photo with a troubled look. "Not that," she said. "Paul knew I didn't actually like the boat, not when he went out in all weather and thought freezing was macho. The problem is Carl...I just hate how he uses Paul, takes advantage. He'd gotten to where he borrowed the boat *a lot*, then Ben started doing it too, taking his cue from Carl. They'd go out together or alone - just call and say, 'hey Paul, okay if I take the boat this weekend?' And he'd say fine, he had work to catch up on. He's always had work to catch up on, especially in the past year since he's more of a plodder than Carl, and hated having the boat just sitting there."

Liddy stopped as something seemed to occur to her. "Maybe, on some level, he saw one or both of them being prospective buyers some day. We were strapped for cash, the boat was a ridiculous expense."

"Still, chutzpah isn't even the word," Kerri said…and thought: So Finn borrowed the boat a lot. Allen too. Which of them could have been out on it that May day with a needy, trusting, maybe by now demanding young coed *who had started to take pictures*; was maybe threatening to go public? Allen's marriage was unraveling; Sasha would make a divorce messier, more expensive. And Carl Finn was dating that hotshot, high earning lawyer…

"Their relationship's more complicated," Liddy was trying to explain. "Paul's also repaying Carl favors from twenty years ago."

Kerri had her notebook back out; scribbled as Liddy told the quick version of their past: Carl the rich kid and Paul his boat boy, desperate for money, thrilled to do every damned chore, help bartend Carl's parties, clean his messes, drive his drunk girl-friends home. Through family pull Carl helped Paul get a full scholarship. "To this day he feels…gratitude isn't even the word."

Kerri was sitting on one of the barstools. "That's a strong history, I get it."

"But there comes a *point*…" Liddy pulled out a barstool too; looked at it; turned away and paced.

"They stayed more or less in touch for years, then resumed big time when Carl discovered they had research in common and he had an in to something exciting – again – through a rich relative. By then Carl had serious hang ups 'cause his father lost every-thing in investments." Liddy stopped pacing; turned. "Win win for Carl! Who better to have back in his life than his forever boat boy - ol' Yessir, nossir, three bags full sir!"

186

Kerri frowned at her ballpoint. "Wait - why did Carl need anyone else for the research?"

"Because two could get it done faster. They got the grant but there's a time limit."

Kerri's phone buzzed and she answered; listened. At the other end a man's voice, and the words *Nicki* and *her friend says Carl something something*. Oddly, Kerri didn't move away with her phone, as if she wanted Liddy to hear.

Disconnecting, she made quick apologies and announced she had to go. "Your grade A intel," she said, pleased. "It's led to a friend of a friend who definitely saw Sasha in Finn's biochem class. She audited briefly, hated it and left, but seems to have made Finn's acquaintance." Kerri started for the door. "The friend of a friend's being interviewed now. This is so good - Nicki alone being a drunk angry ex wouldn't have been enough."

Liddy walked with her, looking apprehensive. "Is Carl going to come charging over here full of accusations?"

"No, we'll still keep you out of the loop." Kerri checked something in her phone. "You've got my number, make sure you've got me on speed dial," she said as she reached for the doorknob. "For anything - either call me directly, or needless to say if it's a bigger emergency, call 9-1-1."

Liddy looked away, newly troubled. Kerri said, "Don't *worry*, your name won't even come up. As long as we have your statement..."

"It's not that."

Liddy's hand went to her brow. "I'm starting to worry about the early symptoms of paranoia because, the whole time we've been talking I've been trying to figure how Beth knew about that fighting couple across the street. I could swear I never told her."

"Call her," Kerri said simply. "She looked tired and pressured – so ambush her, ask how she knew. If she starts going uh, uh instead of being direct, that will tell you something."

Unconsciously, Liddy looked back to the telescope. "I keep hearing what you said about best friends turning out to be not friends at all…" She turned back to Kerri. "Is there *anyone* you ever feel you can trust totally?"

For the first time, Kerri Blasco looked really tired. "Not a question you should ask a cop," she said, but her expression softened. "The thing about best friends? People you trust?" She shrugged. "Even people who presumably care about you can sometimes goof up, speak out of turn, spill something inadvertently you wouldn't want them to. Just be careful. Above all, trust your instincts."

She pointed to the slide bolt and keypad. "Lock up tight." She gave Liddy's arm a squeeze, and left.

43.

Snap went the bolt, punch punch went the keys in the keypad. Then Liddy rested her head against the door, staring down at the door knob.

The wheels were turning.

Worried about the early symptoms of paranoia.

"Did I really say that?" she whispered to herself, though the room behind her suddenly echoed with emptiness and no one was there. "I've been so tired…"

She turned, glanced over for a troubled second at the telescope, and went back to the studio. It pulled her. It was her small safe place where she could at least try to think, and she wanted to see the painting again.

The still-wet paint had drooped, elongating the crying girl's features, making the eyes even more piteous, turning them and the silently pleading mouth down at their corners. A horizontal smear that almost looked like shoulders had started to appear. The mouth seemed almost ready to cry out.

Are hallucinations catching?

Slowly, Liddy sank down to the window seat.

There was no running away from this painting. Its lurid colors had never, not for a second, stopped flashing in Liddy's mind; they had flared and frightened under every word she'd exchanged with Kerri in the kitchen, at the door. Even now, as Liddy stared, the sagging blue eyes seemed to plead to her, above the now nearly dry pigment of *Help Me.*

Too many worries churned.

Had the police gone back to Carl yet? Questioned him given

this new intel as Kerri called it? Maybe not, she was working alone – although that was her partner who called, wasn't it? – but they'd need time to build a new case, dig deeper. Were they now interviewing Nicki's friend of a friend – yes, that's where Kerri had run off to. But accomplishing what? Audits did not exist as documents. Would a judge issue a warrant based on some student's hearsay and an angry ex with a drinking habit? Liddy didn't know much about the law, just had heard of brick walls without number called *circumstantial* blocking requests for judges' warrants. Cops knew that; anyone knew that.

What now?

Liddy looked up to the painting. "I'm so sorry," she breathed to it, feeling helpless tears sting. She turned and stared out at the dusk, the darker fire escape a few feet to the right. She blinked; imagined Carl lunging up and crashing through the window screaming, "Bitch - you put the cops on me after all I've done for you two?"

She shuddered and turned back, hugging herself, rubbing goose bumps on her arms.

Carl crashing through the window – great – now she was having fear dreams awake. Her heart thudded. What to do? Sitting here alone was unbearable, just making worse the *other* worry that kept building.

How had Beth known about the fighting couple?

Liddy got her phone from her pocket; stared stupidly at it. *Ambush her, just ask how she knew*, Kerri said - but she was such a direct person, she'd made it sound so easy. Liddy wasn't direct; she feared hurting, offending, alienating…someone she loved would stop loving her, it was a childish old fear she'd never shaken. So she sat, like a scared, witless dummy as her mind fumbled for words - until finally, the tightening knot in her chest and watching the room's shadows close in forced her finger, slowly, to hit speed dial.

"Hey!" boomed Beth's voice, quick and hurried answering on the first ring. "You beat me to it. I was going to call you."

"Oh?" Sounds of traffic at the other end, a car door slamming, probably a cab.

"To *confess*. I'm an idiot and I hate myself." Higher-voiced: "West Broadway and Broome, please." Back to the phone: "I felt guilty the second I left you – in case there was something you noticed."

"The couple fighting across the street?" The words tumbled out.

"Argh, yes, it's been so bothering me. I knew about that because Paul called me, upset because you were upset. He told me what you saw, said it shook him more than he let on to you because he wanted you to calm, not feel so fretful about everything. He said he didn't know where to turn."

"He was worried? He should have told me."

"That's what *I* told him. Oh boy, wait a sec." Beth's voice rose trying to explain where she wanted to go to a driver who didn't speak English. "No, *West* Broadway, not Broadway-Broadway. It's on the corner of Broome Street. *Broome Street, Broome Street!*"

Back to the phone: "I gotta confess more. Paul called me a second time, like, two days ago, I think - I forget, can't even remember what today is."

"Paul called you again?" Liddy's lips parted.

"Yes. Oh definitely two days ago, I was in the middle of the Whitley open house. That second time...he started out funny, beating around the bush, saying how stressed he was that Carl was stressed they weren't going fast enough. Again, he said he didn't want to bring his worries to you, you had enough to deal with - and again, I told him no, he *should* share. Isn't that what marriage is supposed to be?"

"Yes."

"He went on and on about Carl, and the fact that he was worried...God..."

191

"About what?"

"That you were focused too *much* on Carl, imagining bad things about him. And he asked me…oh Lids, I've been wanting to tell you…"

"Tell me now." Liddy's voice shook.

"He asked if I'd report on your - fever chart, that's what he called it…to please tell him if you were saying anything about Carl that sounded…Jesus…"

"Paranoid?" The heart, racing…

"In so many words, yes. I got mad, told him it sounded like he wanted me to *spy* on you. I wanted to tell you but I couldn't, you've been upset enough." A horn blared at Beth's end; someone shouted, then her voice dropped lower. "Frankly, I think there's something wrong with those two dudes' relationship. It seems like Carl puts Paul *up* to things, dominates him…"

"No kidding."

"…the feeling I got from that second call was Paul feeling - like, frantic, pulled into some kind of web of Carl's - who come to think of it may have even *told* Paul to call me. Am I wrong? *Something's* going on with them."

"Paul's been cleaning up Carl's messes for years."

"Or *covering* up. You don't think-"

"I don't know. I'm so glad you told me."

"Of course! I hope I haven't upset you too much. Listen sweetie, I'll be *in in in* tonight. If you have even a smidgen of a bad moment, call me, okay?"

"I will. Speak soon, Beth."

Liddy hung up.

Last night, last awful night, the thought had come to her: Even if Paul suspected Carl of something, he'd still cover up…

Now what?

It was nine minutes after seven.

For a moment in the darkened room Liddy faced the painting's eyes, sharing their sorrow. Outside, thunder rumbled. She got up and went for her slicker, put her phone in her handbag, but not her sketchbook. No, for once that stayed. She went down the hall and through the living room, carefully setting the slide bolt and alarm system, closing the door behind her. Halfway down the stairs, she passed a delivery boy carrying up a pizza box. She hadn't eaten; barely noticed it.

On Prince Street she got a taxi.

44.

A white-coated assistant at the front counter smiled. She smiled tensely back as she walked the aisle past grad students still working at more counters until she saw a Winnie the Pooh, a big one with a big tummy under his red T-shirt, and asked the tired student about it.

"Carl gave it to me," the student beamed with the overhead fluorescents making her glasses look like headlights, and the headlights reminded Liddy of her accident, the onrushing, frantic car blaring wildly. "Wasn't that sweet of him?" the student beamed. "He said a little girl gave it to him."

Liddy said yes, that was sweet, and continued to Paul and Carl's long counter at the end.

Carl looked up from poking a white mouse. His face turned fake jovial. "Hey, surprise! Back so soon?"

"Just stopping by." Liddy kept her voice even; pointed shakily to the mouse to duck further exchange. "Is it alive?" The little thing was on its back with its four legs stretched out in all directions. Carl's gloved hand held a scalpel.

"Yep, just paralyzed briefly," he said, bending back with his scalpel. "Watch, I'll cut-"

"Don't!" Her tension showed, but she let him think it was her usual dislike of what they did. "Is Paul around?" she asked – just as he emerged from the office behind the counter, white-coated, carrying a clipboard in one gloved hand and a small cage holding one mouse in the other.

"Lids. Hey." He acted surprised too, and set the cage down. The mouse bore red markings on its white fur, which meant the scratching little thing wasn't long for this world. Liddy looked at it, thinking *doomed, doomed,* then looked back to Paul, who watched her expectantly.

"I need to talk to you," she said.

"Now, Lids?" He didn't hide his impatience. "This is a big moment, big *big*." He pointed to Carl's sedated mouse. "What we just used will keep her out for five minutes, shorter and better than Propofol. Look, Carl just made a cut and she didn't even twitch! How 'bout that?" he grinned at Carl, who nodded jubilantly but didn't look up from reaching for sutures to stitch Mouse's little incision.

"Three minutes ten seconds so far," Carl said, checking his watch. "In less than two more minutes this critter's going to be back to crawling around, hurting and really pissed at me. Hey, she gets to live another day!"

"Congrats," Liddy said dryly, seeing that Paul's eyes were now fixed on her: *What gives? You hate to come here.*

Her answer was to turn and step into their office: twin desks facing each other in a room filled with computers, papers, monitor screens showing mouse brain cross-sections, and a few empty cages. A closed door with a red EXIT sign led out to a hall.

Liddy leaned on Paul's desk to face him.

"I have a question," she said, inhaling hard, folding her arms tight.

"Shoot." He sensed this was going someplace unpleasant, because his face tightened and he half-closed the door.

Quietly, she asked, "Would you be able to work separately? Minus *him*?" She cocked her head toward the door.

Paul blinked and frowned. "What?"

"You're just as brilliant as he is. That latest drug composition is yours, isn't it? Your formula?"

"Well yeah – after a thousand other tries working together. What gives?"

She turned away from him, still with her arms folded. "Your work is done. You've got your formula or whatever you call it, the grant people will be thrilled and" – she turned, pointed to the door - "he'll be rich in prison."

"Liddy..."

"You have to save yourself," she whispered desperately. "Cut ties professionally. Are you not *aware* of his tightening connection to Sasha Perry?"

Paul hesitated, then held up both palms. "Yes. We've talked more about it and it's bullshit."

"You've-"

"After Righetti's. He says there's nothing there. Please, Liddy-"

"He had a *fling* with her. *Something* connecting those two is what's been making me crazy. Please, you have to get away *for my* sake-"

"Oh Lids, what's happening again?" He tried to reach for her; she cringed away. "I really, really fear for your mind-"

"Now who's talking bullshit?" Liddy cried. "She's *dead*, Paul. Sasha Perry is dead, the cops are closing in on Carl, you'd cover for him even if you suspected - and *you don't care about me*." Tears literally burst from her eyes and she turned for the exit. "Okay, I tried. I'm outta here."

Paul grabbed her wrist and held tight. "Control yourself," he growled.

She whirled on him. "Why? Because *you* tell me to? You who don't care what's in front of you and don't give a damn about-"

The door opened. Carl came in, his lips pressed tight; saw Paul holding on to Liddy with her trying to break his grip.

"Knock it off," he said.

Paul looked at him; let go just like that. Liddy saw the two of them trade glances. Something was happening here; something strange as Carl's expression turned regretful; looked at Liddy.

"Yes," he said quietly. "Something – nobody knows what -

seems to have happened to that girl." Then he held up his thumb and index finger, a half inch apart. "But we're this close to the least dangerous surgical anesthetic ever developed-"

"Great." Liddy backed away. "You'll get the Nobel *and* the chair-"

"-and this girl...Sasha...was troubled. Again, nobody knows what happened to her, so I beg you, don't let progress like we're making-"

"*You* know what happened to her!" Liddy shot back, weeping. "You hide behind your white coat and think you're immune, but you're not – and *Paul's done covering for you!*"

Carl blinked; looked at her for a long moment. Then raised his hands in surrender, his eyes sorry as he looked back to Paul.

"I tried," he said. "We've both tried, and I'm tired. Isn't it time to tell your wife that this is *your mess?* I really don't want the cops back again questioning *me.*"

He shook his head and left, closing the door behind him.

Liddy stood motionless, paralyzed.

"*Your* mess?" she breathed.

"Lids..."

Like an explosion, the memory flashed back.

"I know," she whimpered. "I was there, before the accident. *She* was there, in our old apartment... Sasha... You tried to lie, say you were just helping her cope after Carl dropped her – and she looked at you so hurt, started crying, 'But you said you love *me.*'"

"Liddy." He reached and she yanked away, backed around the desk.

"I came home," she wept. "You'd both been...what? Skinny dipping? Her hair was wet."

"Wet? What are you *talking* about? That's not what happened!"

Liddy backed toward the exit. "Sasha looked at me, I remember now. Her blue shirt was wet – *that's* how I remember a blue shirt...and she looked *sorry.*"

197

She flung open the door and was out, careening into grad students who turned in the hall as Paul caught up to her, seized her wrist again but she ripped free.

"Please, I tried to stop you."

"I ran into the street, saw the headlights, kept running-"

"Forgive, I'd been trying to break it off," he begged as she burst through the heavy front door, started down the cement steps with him at her heels. "She fell too hard for me, threatened to go to the dean, wreck everything we'd worked for, threaten *us*. She was unstable, *hooked on uppers Carl gave her-*"

Liddy spun on him. "Uppers Carl-?" She almost laughed. "You took Carl's castoff, then bitched she fell too hard for you? What *are* women to you creeps? Just toys to play with and lie to?"

She signaled a cab that pulled over. Paul was desperate, pleading. "I was a fool, out of my mind. I made a mistake."

"Go to hell. You never said a word to help me understand the accident."

"So you'd run into the traffic again? Jesus, forgive, I didn't know what to do!"

His words were lost as the cab door slammed, and she was gone.

45.

*t*hrub *a-dub hissss*
   higher hiss, soft…like a far radio frequency…
   Low steady ring ring ring…
These sounds in the ears: better with the eyes closed.

Sometimes the sounds faded, and then there was only pain, the heart pulverized yet still somehow able to be astonished, just amazed at its own stupidity. Angry, too. Oh yes, very angry at the good old stupidity. How much easier it is to live in the soft, blurry warmth of one's own ignorance…

She opened her eyes and asked that question – silently – of the Striped One. What was it called? Wait, the mind wasn't working yet, was refusing to work…oh yes, it's called angelfish, see it drift languidly through the water, its fins barely moving, without stress, so without stress, its snout down, pecking delicately through wafting grasses at flakes specially formulated…but here comes another angel, and a third one and look, they're getting aggressive with each other. C'mon, guys, this tank isn't big enough for you? Beth said they get more territorial as they get older; they fight, even these slow beauties now still young enough to glide away from each other, wander elsewhere in this carefully tended, soft-bubbling world.

"You calming?"

Beth's voice came from somewhere. Into her limp hands something warm was placed, and she felt Beth's hands wrap her fingers around it. Liddy looked down at the mug of hot cocoa. She squeezed it.

"Mm-m. Thanks."

"Can't beat the two of them, hot cocoa and especially the aquarium." Beth plunked onto the couch behind Liddy; let out a pained breath. "I swear by aquariums to relieve stress, they're mesmerizing, right up there with staring into a fire in the fireplace with glowing embers beneath the logs. Only who in Manhattan has working fireplaces with glowing embers – who even has *logs*? Except for decoration…you burn your expensive-in-the-city logs and then they're gone, no woodshed. So for here aquariums win."

"The bubbling sound alone…"

"Yeah, nice. Almost beats Valium." Liddy could hear Beth plumping throw pillows, muttering that they'd been losing their feathers. Then Beth said, "Take deep, slow breaths, hear nothing but the bubbling. Emotional closeout! Everything must go! No pain or static allowed."

"I'm going to start calling you Yoda."

"Ha."

Beth's apartment was open, with few walls and the long, turquoise-hued aquarium acting like a room divider. Very Feng Shui, really nice. Liddy had seen party guests gravitate to the aquarium, oohing and pointing and forgetting themselves. It was hard to wrench herself away but she did; finally left the chair she'd pulled up to the fish and returned with her cocoa to the couch. Beth was now fiddling with an old-fashioned afghan.

"Crocheting helps too," she murmured, fingering soft wool strands of orange and peach. "I made this during the split from Rob. It saved me from killing myself."

"You told me." Liddy put her mug next to where she'd left her phone on the coffee table. "Gotta buy me some yarn."

They fell silent for a long moment. Liddy just stared at her mug. Beth patted the afghan, then took another deep, consoling breath. "But really, I gotta be fair," she said slowly, catching Liddy's look and raising her hands. "No, it has to be said - the split from Rob only came after *more* of his screwing around. In retrospect, I would have been happy with that once."

"You don't mean that."

"Okay, maybe not when it happened and I was so girly hurt, betrayed, crying and throwing things, but later I realized…that first time had too much to do with my pride, and we healed after that – remember him bringing flowers, going all rose-nutty, filling every room and the bathroom with flowers?"

"Guilt. Overdoing it."

"True. I knew it but like your standard chump it placated me – and made him feel off the hook and then he went back to his tricks, and I just got sick of him – frankly stopped giving a damn, stopped trying to love him. That's what did it, the accumulation of…" Her voice trailed.

"Lies," Liddy finished for her.

"Right, but multiple lies, deceptions, squirming like a spineless worm. Something else? Despite all the damn flowers and the gold bracelet Rob never said Sorry – not once, apology wasn't in him. Whereas *this*…" Beth shook her head, peered across to the fish for help. "I can't even believe it. Paul has always seemed crazy about you. At the hospital he was in such bad shape, terrified of losing you."

Liddy looked to the fish too; frowned. "Why do men cheat?"

A who-the-hell-knows gesture. "Because they're wired that way? Or, they like to be bad? In Paul's case, 'cause Carl had his fun in the toy store and Paul wanted some too? He may have figured, no harm if no one knows, this little girl gets around anyway."

Liddy's cell phone buzzed. She just stared at it on the coffee table. Beth reached for it and checked the readout.

"Paul again. This makes his fourth call."

"Ignore."

"He doesn't even know where you are."

Liddy shook her head, back and forth. "Lying by omission...big omission...is also lying." Her voice was bitter. "He let me go through months of nightmares, lost sleep...never once tried to explain the accident."

Beth inhaled, solemn. "He was afraid you'd 'run back into the traffic?' That's what he said?"

Nod.

"He may have meant it literally. Either way he was terrified of your reaction." Beth touched Liddy's arm. "Hey," she said. "He's frantic. You two had a bad fight, he doesn't know where you are, and last time you got really upset you wound up spending four days in intensive care. Let me call him back at least, tell him you're okay. Sleep here tonight. Sleep on the whole thing...tomorrow you may feel different." Beth tried to smile. "That sound okay? A chance for you both to simmer down?"

For long moments Liddy glared at her phone.

"Okay," she finally said.

46.

The Skype connection was bad. Twice it dropped, and when it came back the sound and image were distorted and the screen was red.

"Crappy connection, huh?" said the man in the screen.

"Yes, sorry," Kerri Blasco said. "Now I hear you but you sound like Darth Vader."

"You look yellow at my end."

"Wait a sec? Our brilliant technician here is fixing cables. Old cables. Your taxpayer dollars at work."

"Tell me about it."

Jerry the tech guy made his adjustments, and the thirtyish, sweet-faced man in his camouflage Air National Guard uniform came into focus.

"Ah, better."

"You look better, too. You're pretty."

"You must be sleepy. I really appreciate this, the hour's ungodly where you are."

He smiled and shrugged. "Four-thirty in Kabul. We get up at five anyway. How can I help?"

Peter Dunn, his name was. He was a New York City EMT and a sergeant volunteering his second tour of duty in Afghanistan. He'd been on some assignment and was finally, after nine days, reachable for Kerri. She'd already emailed him her question: Did he by any chance remember the hit-and-run accident on last June third, at three in the morning in front of 410 West 83rd?

He did. Emailed back that, in fact, the accident still bothered him, still seemed weird, he'd never gotten it out of his mind.

203

"Busy night, but some things you just remember," he wrote. They'd made an appointment to Skype – by five local he'd have to roll – and now here they were.

"I spoke to your partner Doug." Kerri gave a quick smile of thanks to the tech leaving. She had her notebook out and her ballpoint ready. "He only remembers the injury but used the same word you did – weird – about there being more to that accident. He couldn't remember what."

"Well, that night…" Peter's sensitive eyes looked into the screen. "Doug's doing better. He's…"

"Out of rehab, yes, doing great. Volunteer teaching kids about drug and alcohol abuse."

"We Skype. I helped him white-knuckle it." Peter glanced down to the table before him and clasped his hands; then he looked back to the screen. "So, that accident was something. Head trauma, a broken rib and the leg a really messy compound, comminuted fracture - under the lights you could see it from fifteen feet away, the bone all splintered and sticking right through her jeans. Awful."

Kerri had researched Liddy Barron's accident; now picked up one of two printouts before her. "The police report just lists the accident's bare details, the felony hit and run, and catching the drunk driver minutes later. There's nothing here suggesting what you and Doug felt about something weird - only that the injured woman ran right into the path of the oncoming car. The officer writing up the report said it looked like she was trying to kill herself."

"Definitely," Peter nodded. "Like I said, it was awful."

"Was the husband there?"

"No, and that was the first, *less* strange thing. He came running out just after we arrived, hysterical, telling the cops he'd been looking all over for her. I heard and thought that was ridiculous - hell, if you live in a New York apartment, how much looking do you have to do?

I don't think the cop questioning him thought it odd, but I did."

"Anything else you noticed about the husband?"

Peter frowned slightly at something off camera, remembering. "They'd both been drinking – you have that?"

"Only Ms Barron's blood alcohol, zero point one three."

Peter looked back, raised his eyebrows. "*He* reeked too. It seemed pretty clear they'd been drinking and fighting. He insisted on coming in the ambulance – understandable – but that's when I noticed the second strange thing – what really made me remember."

"What?" Kerri sat forward, suddenly breathing and scribbling faster.

"The unconscious woman's hair was wet. Rather, still damp as if it had *been* wet. I was curious, so I felt her collar. Also damp, and her jeans. The cops wouldn't have noticed 'cause it was us cutting her clothes off. It just seemed strange - who has damp hair *and* clothes at three in the morning?"

"And goes tearing out into traffic," Kerri muttered, scribbling madly, thinking - a water connection!

"Weird like that you remember," Peter said, shaking his head as if still seeing the accident.

Behind Kerri the door opened and Alex came in, hearing that last comment, sitting next to her out of picture range where the tech guy had been. He leaned and started reading her notes. She was concentrating intensely, but she felt his surprised glance.

"What about the husband's hair and clothes?" she asked Peter Dunn. "Also wet?"

"Hard to say – his hair looked either damp or sweaty, it was a hot night and he was sitting on the opposite bench. I couldn't very well reach across the ambulance to feel his shirt."

"But you wanted to?" Kerri was clutching her pen so hard that her fingers cramped.

"I'll say. It bugged me later that I didn't mention what I saw to the cops."

"Ha, you know what you would have gotten at that hour?" Kerri put down her pen and grimaced in pain, trying to straighten her bent fingers. She heard Alex snicker. Seven thousand miles away, Peter also saw and cracked a smile.

"You just made me feel better," he said. "Yeah, cops are in wonderful moods at three in the morning. They would have told me to just do my damned job and don't bleeping complicate things. The scene was pretty chaotic…then days later things got crazy 'cause I had to get ready for this." Peter gestured around him. The clock behind him read four fifty-six.

Kerri said, "I can't thank you enough. You've given me a new slant on this case."

Peter Dunn smiled. "Hey, I'm relieved. Three months later and it still nagged." Somewhere in the background a buzzer sounded. "Oops, gotta go. Good luck with it."

"And you, Peter. Thanks again and stay safe!"

"I'll try. It was nice talking to you. Makes me less homesick."

The screen went blank. Kerri fell back in her chair, letting out a huge, pent-up breath. Alex reached for her notebook and flipped pages, stopping where her handwriting got crazy excited.

He pointed. "Wet? Liddy Barron's hair was damp from *being* wet? That's something."

"Another water connection and a big one." Kerri felt suddenly drained. "It means something…but what? I'll go back over her files, the hospital report, witness statements, swill caffeine extra strong to re-stoke the blown gray cells… Am I stuttering? Making sense?" She saw Alex was looking at her funny, smiling. "What?"

"Your hair. It's cute like that, half in and half out of its ponytail."

"Fix it. Put an ice pack on my head while you're at it."

He leaned back, used both hands to pull her hair back into its band. They were alone in the control room with its monitors and floor cables. He pulled close again, and kissed her cheek. His warmth, the soft scrape of his stubble…the comfort felt so good. Tension started to drain away, Kerri turned her face to him, and they kissed, long and tenderly.

"I'll help you," he whispered. "Together we can-"

"Stop. Kiss me again."

He did.

Then he said, "Do this at your place? Home is better. Can I sleep over?"

"Yes, my bed has so missed you." She dropped her brow wearily to his. He cupped her cheek with a warm, strong hand.

"I've stuff to finish here, can be at your place in an hour. Don't make the coffee too strong."

"Okay."

47.

Key in the lock, done.

Open door, done.

Punch keyboard buttons, lock up again, done. Her hand shook just a little.

Liddy turned to face the apartment. Everything was gray. Gloomy gray light came in from the early dusk, no shadows, even the white columns looked gray.

She didn't feel afraid; didn't feel much, actually. In this long, long day something in her had turned to lead. He told Beth he'd be here, would go to work then be back early - but the place was nearly dark. There was a musty feeling to it too, no coffee or cooking smells. Paul could make eggs at least – and here it was after seven and the place was like a mausoleum. How fitting, she thought. She had lain awake until almost seven this morning, then had slept at last and slept late, waking to find Beth's note – "Decaf! Just press da button!" - and Beth's key duplicates and a pile of pastries in the kitchen.

But she'd barely eaten. Had gone back to bed in Beth's small guest bedroom, pulled the blanket up around her, and lain and thought. For hours, lying still, she'd let her mind float free. Tried to, anyway.

Sasha's faces, all of them, kept coming back to her. Alive, smiling and happy online. Then weeping in the mist before the plants, and in the shower stall; then the eyes, most of all, mournful and begging to her with *Help me* scrawled beneath.

Had Paul seen the painting? Gone into the studio? Oh God…

Liddy switched on the lamp by the door, then the Victorian

glass lamp by the couch, glancing down, for a moment, at the DVD of *Vampire Island*, remembering the night they had watched it. Rather, the night she had watched it. Paul had gotten almost immediately antsy and jumped up, walked away. Couldn't bear watching someone dying and begging for help, even if just on film.

Remembering that night was one of the things she'd kept coming back to, lying in Beth's bed. It should have seemed like a small thing…but it wasn't.

A sound from the bedroom. The mattress creaked, then footsteps approached, and there he was.

Paul, standing uncertainly in the dimness of the hall, looking suddenly thin, very thin, unshaven with dark circles under his eyes. He was dressed in a wrinkled oxford shirt and dark pants; shoes, too. So he'd gone to work, come back to bed but never took off his shoes? Or had he just put them back on?

"Liddy." His voice was a croak.

She said nothing; went to turn on the second lamp on the side of the couch near him. This close, his appearance scared her, started her heart thudding. His eyes were lost dark wells, darker still in the hall where he still stood, fixed on her.

Absurdly, having no words, she said the first thing she would have normally said. "Have you eaten?"

Vague nod. "At work. Came home early."

"Did you sleep?"

"No."

He went to her, his arms out to embrace her. She let him. He hadn't showered. He was trembling, squeezing her, mumbling about his relief, his sorrow. "Never again," he kept saying. "…don't know where my mind was. The stress, the research, the flattery from some kid when I was scared of failure."

Some kid. He had toyed with her and she was just some kid…

Liddy's heart pounded harder. After long seconds she pulled away; made herself look at him dead on. "Before anything," she said shakily, "I need to know. Did you have anything to do with Sasha's disappearance?"

"God, no." He turned away, headed back up the hall. "It was a mistake, an insane mistake. I beg you, can we put it in our past?"

Nothing about the painting. He hadn't been in the studio.

There was more Liddy had to ask him. Things that had come to her at Beth's.

She followed him into the dark, musty bedroom that smelled of sweat. Not the old sweat of gyms, but new sweat – lots of it. She bent and felt Paul's pillow. Damp. Ditto his sheets. He was pacing, a dark silhouette on the other side of the bed. Liddy straightened; faced him across the bed that seemed as dark and wide as a battlefield at night. She didn't turn on the lamp.

"So you ended it," she said unsteadily.

"Yes." His silhouette turned; paced the other way. There were maybe four feet between that side of the bed and the window. His body was hunched, as if wanting to run, but he was stuck in his little alley over there.

Another question rose that had nagged the whole afternoon at Beth's. Liddy looked across their dark battlefield, and inhaled. "We spent four years in the old apartment, didn't we?"

The silhouette looked briefly toward her; looked away, paced. "Yes," he answered again, but in a tone that said, What of it?

"It was actually four and a *half* years, during which I always wanted to move, and you didn't."

"The recession. It was a big place for a good price. A good deal."

"It didn't stop being a good deal. Yet after my accident, why were you suddenly in such a rush to move - you even went looking with Beth *before* I could walk, see places for myself. Why was that?"

The silhouette stopped, spread its hands, took a ragged breath. "Because I loved you. Wanted you to be happy."

"And *not remember the night of the accident?* I'd lost my memory – a stroke of luck for you-"

"*No.*" He came toward her again. She wheeled back out to the dark hall, crossed to her studio, felt around frantically for her tensor lamp. He was on her heels in the dimness, pleading that he'd known she'd always wanted Soho. "Frankly I felt guilty for being a tightwad."

"Although you kept the boat, the really expensive boat."

"It was my father's, it was all he *had*." Shakily she got the lamp on as he tripped over her tall stool, righted it and himself and just stood there, breathing hard, looking desperate. "Lids, for God's sake…"

She backed away. Her heart whammed and her leg ached. "You got worried when you saw my memory starting to return – then, oh didn't you work fast! You thought this glorious move with all its" – her hands flew up – "*busyness* would take my mind permanently off seeing you and Sasha-"

"No…." He stepped pleadingly toward her as she backed away further, close to her shelves. Peripherally she saw her box cutter, inches away.

"I want you," she said bitterly, "to tell me what happened that night. *I have to know,*" she cried, her finger jabbing like a crazy person's to her chair before her work table. "Sit. Tell me," she ordered.

He gave up. Fell to the chair like a marionette whose strings have been cut; dropped his sweaty brow to his hand. Behind him, glowing, the painting he hadn't seen. The face was different; the eyes glared down at him.

"I…" Paul's voice was thin, desperate. "…couldn't let you know, because if you did…"

"I'd what? Turn you in? Wreck your life and your prestigious research?" Liddy inched closer to her box cutter; noticed – oh God - that her long scissors were still on her work table behind

Paul. She feared him seeing them so she pointed jerkily to the door. "That bedroom you spent hours in *smells of guilt.* You were sweating buckets of guilt, weren't you?"

He was shaking his head, his head that was still in his hand. "Not guilt," he rasped, very quietly...and suddenly the room stilled, became quiet as death.

Paul looked up at her, his eyes stricken. "I was sweating fear." He inhaled, then plunged as if his next words would finish them both. "Fear you'd remember...that you killed Sasha."

48.

She just stared at him, for long, ticking seconds.

"You bastard," she finally whispered.

His head was back in his hands, but he seemed quieter now; resigned. His free hand gripped her chair arm.

"What you were crying about at the lab," he said softly, "that Sasha and I had been…skinny dipping? Her hair was wet?" He looked sorrowfully at the floor. "It was *your* hair that was wet," he whispered, then stopped dead silent.

Liddy's heart racketed so loud she could hear it.

"Remember now?" he said after a bit. "Did I just jog the rest?"

After everything, everything, the thought that he would play this final, hideous trick on her took her breath away, and suddenly a longing dragged at Liddy to do nothing but collapse, to surrender completely before such evil. She withstood it though; shut her eyes tight for a second, then pulled together all her resolve and hatred too; hatred for this man she'd never really known who had put her and was still putting her through such horror. Fast, she reached for her box cutter; flicked the blade out to its longest; held it firmly point-down at her side.

Insanely, Paul didn't react. Just sat there, looking sad. "Another death, Liddy? Okay, go for it. Without me to cover for you, what will you do this time?"

She gripped her blade tighter, trembling. "I never went near Sasha."

He stared limply at the floor. "You came back from that gallery opening and found us. Found us fighting, ironically. She just…showed up because I'd been trying to break it off. She'd

213

been pleading and crying, hanging on me when you walked in." Paul looked up. "Does that bring it back? DiStefano's gallery opening? You'd been drinking, came home holding a half empty champagne bottle and threw it at me."

"No," Liddy breathed. Then, like a flash, part of it did come. Her knees buckled. Her back hit the wall and she slid slowly to the floor. "You told Sasha…'Wait for me in the boat'…I heard you say that." Her face crumpled; an angry tear spilled down her cheek.

He rose from the chair and knelt to her, held her shoulders. "No," he said gently. "'Wait for me in the boat' is *what you texted her* - from my phone later while I slept." He looked down at the blade she still gripped; tried to ease it from her. She wrenched her hand from him and raised it, glaring and threatening. He held his hands up in surrender.

"Okay," he said softly. "Keep it. Just listen." But one hand dropped close to hers, ready to grab.

"I heard the door close when you left." His eyes grieved. "We'd been fighting and drinking after she ran out. I thought you'd left me and I just…lay there, miserable. Then it occurred to check my phone…" He gulped air. "*I ran.* Wasn't in time. You were in the water. She was…gone."

His free hand reached to brush a strand of hair from her brow; his other hand stayed near hers gripping her blade. "I got you out, soaking. I walked us back. Didn't even want a cab to see."

Liddy gaped at him, struggling to breathe, tears of shock streaming.

Paul pulled her to him, comforting, comforting, again trying to take her blade, again giving in to her resistance. "Did you take one of my anesthetics with you? Find her in bed and knock her out? You drowned her, Liddy. Weighted her down with something, let the current carry her off, that's what you said. You even sent her phone down with her. All the way home you ranted,

'See? I thought of everything.'" He exhaled hard. "It was almost three in the morning. You were still...crazed, fighting with me, drinking more when we got back. Then you...ran out."

"Into the traffic," Liddy wept, gripping her blade.

"Yes."

"Wh-what about *your* phone? If I texted her..."

"I erased it."

He pulled her to him again. "Shh...they'll never know. The girl was self-destructive, and we've been through a bad patch. What happened is out now between us, but they'll never know. We're going to be okay."

Liddy looked up to the painting, saw the eyes.

"I remember now," she breathed, tears slowing, finally seeing every image of that terrible night flashing, resurfacing. "You brought it all back."

"Yes."

"Only, you told it backwards."

He looked at her. "What?"

"You told what *you* did, and *I* followed. You were drunk when I got you out of the water, ranting she was going to go to the dean, ruin you. You'd swum out with her, let the current take her. No one would know, you kept saying. They'll never find her."

Paul dropped back on his haunches and stared at her. "Oh Lids, now what?"

"She agrees." Liddy pointed up to the painting.

He turned, saw Sasha Perry glaring down at him, the words *Help me* beneath.

"You painted that!" He looked incredulously back at her. "You painted it like that!"

"No, Sasha came to me. She's been begging me for help."

"My God, have you really-"

"You killed her."

He saw her move. Her hands shook wildly as she tried to hang

215

on to her cutter and get out her phone - *hit speed dial, call Kerri* – but with a yell he was on her like a wild man, one hand crushing her wrist holding the blade, the other hand flinging her phone away. No, God, please…she heard it clunk something and skitter away; knew she was dead as she struggled against his weight, screaming "You killed her, you killed her!" but he was on her face fast, pressing an acrid-smelling cloth. *No!* His better-than-Propofol, *he'd had it all along!* Had just been playing her, knew she'd never stay silent, was probably planning to – what? – drown her in the bathtub? Say she'd been suicidal?

She felt the drug's first effects, started to paralyze but her eyes still moved…and then froze, gaping in horror at what she saw behind him.

49.

*P*_{ing!}

The oddest feeling came to her, just like that, as Kerri waited for the mess to clear on Broadway. Maybe a reflex – the car in front of her had screeched to a stop, hadn't made it through the yellow light and now was out there, in the middle of the intersection at 72nd, blocking traffic from everywhere. Instant jam, with horns blasting, people leaning out shouting. Great, just the thing for her head pounding with weariness, her blown fuse of a mind still struggling with what Peter Dunn had told her.

Liddy Barron's hair and clothes, damp as if they'd *been* wet. Again, the damned water connection…key to her every nightmare, hallucination – and that painting! She'd swooshed her brushes through more water than pigment; had been in too much of a frenzy to notice the colors dripping, dripping.

"What does it mean?" Kerri whispered to herself, watching uniformed cops waving madly, shouting and pointing, getting things moving again. The car in front of her started to inch forward. She did too, her left hand on the steering wheel, her right hand reaching to push back her laptop that had slid forward.

Ping!

She felt it again, straight to her heart as she touched the laptop. She frowned; it was the strangest feeling, like something pulling at her.

Then her phone buzzed; she grabbed it.

"You killed her, you killed her!" she heard and froze; checked the readout.

Liddy Barron's phone. Sounds of a struggle, another scream and a loud thump, like a body flung down.

Kerri's blood ran cold. She called it in.

"Dispatch, send available units to 290 Prince Street, assault in progress." Her heart was exploding. "Yes, assault in progress!" she said again. "Tell 'em to break the door down - if they hear nothing tell 'em *I* heard a cry for help."

She popped the top hat onto her roof and hit the siren. *Whoop whoop!* it went. Every uniform looked her way and nodded, pulled cars over, made room. She executed a quick U-turn and raced back down Broadway, hunched not breathing at the wheel, careening and zig-zagging around cabs and cars, barely missing a pulled-over van.

Her radio crackled with urgency. She heard dispatch get blue-and-whites to clear the way ahead, lead her faster.

It took her till 48th Street to get her breath half back; call Alex; tell him to head for Liddy's too.

50.

Paul leaped to his feet as Sasha's face focused, came to life and rose out at him, dead and withered but raging. His eyes widened as he screamed, stumbled back, crushed a lamp falling and hit his head.

The room fell into shadows.

Liddy's body was encased in cement, but her mind still worked. And her eyes – she could gape right, left, see Paul's darkened form lying feet away, dark blood near his head. She'd be paralyzed...for how long? Under five minutes, they said.

She saw Paul stir.

Sasha was back in her painting.

Liddy fixed her frantic eyes on the dead girl. *Help me*, she implored, but Sasha was back to gazing mournfully down at her. *I died too*, her eyes seemed to say. Liddy felt stinging tears of despair. Her mind strained at every muscle, fighting. How many minutes since he'd pressed that cloth to her face? More than one; two, probably. She didn't know, she was reeling. For long seconds, she gave up. Lay there, crying and screaming inside. This couldn't be happening - no, she'd been through too much; had struggled bravely through too much. She could breathe, at least, though shallowly. A great drug, really; it left you breathing and thinking, you just couldn't move.

Now she knew she was really gone, dead and defeated because her sanity had let go, gone giddy-crazy with a sudden feeling of gratefulness because breathing really was something, wasn't it? What an underrated function! We ought to bow down every day and give thanks just for breathing! Go around with smiley faces telling others to have a nice breathe! She struggled to pull in a deeper breath. Managed half way. Then did another, that time feeling her shoulders raise ever so slightly to enable the best breath yet.

Her shoulders raised...? She tried that again, got resistance...then again with less resistance. Inhaled deep and hard with something close to a gasp.

Just as Paul's foot near her moved.

But she could move her foot, too! Which started her heart racing in terrifying hope: she could move her foot and oh my God twitch her fingers! It was wearing off...*hurry*. The phone. He'd thrown it, she hadn't been able to hit that one pathetic, little life-saving button for speed dial. The room was in near darkness. Where had he thrown it?

More cement gave way and she was able to roll over. Crawl. Inch her way toward the dim outline of door, having trouble keeping her head up, neck muscles still not cooperating. Her heart whammed. She got her hand out, out further; found the door. That *clunk!* when he threw it came from here, sounded like it hit the jamb, maybe ricocheted out. Her fingers were working now, groping over wood floor, feeling through shadows. She crawled out to the darker hall.

A sound.

She heard him move in the studio, hit with a *clink* the lamp he'd knocked over.

He was up. The phone, the phone! Her fingers scrabbled. She could move better now; she just couldn't see...too dark in the hall and he was coming after her, stumbling, toppling more things from the sound of it. Something crashed, then something else. She crawled faster to get away – and her hand hit her phone. Oh dear God, saved maybe? She grasped it, her hands shaking in convulsive terror – and the phone slipped away again. Just inches away it skidded, she could see it glint-

Too late, he was on her, throwing himself and half falling on her, growling, "Bitch...tried to destroy me..." but he was disoriented, one hand trying to get his acrid cloth back on her face, his other hand crushing her throat, putting all his weight on her throat as she kicked, wrenched away, seized the phone back up into her fingers which groped in the dark and...

Paul screamed.

Liddy got her head around; gaped.

Above him, Sasha, a bright silver mist of withered-faced fury, an all-bones arm up and then down as she plunged the long scissors into his back. Another, higher scream and he fell, face down, his back a spreading stain of dark centered by the glinting scissor rings.

Sasha looked at Liddy, her misted features changing from fury to peace, even something approaching a tragic smile. Then her silvery shape receded, disappeared.

Liddy lay gasping, blinking incredulously toward the door. "Sasha," she whispered feebly; then with every last ounce of her strength, she raised her voice as if in prayer. "Sasha, thank you."

From the direction of the studio came a sound. Indecipherable at first, then unmistakable. Gentle and sweet, the sound of singing.

Liddy crawled; found her phone. Her numb fingers shook as she finally hit 9-1-1.

"They're almost there," a voice said. "You already called."

"No...I didn't."

"Well *someone* did."

Liddy didn't understand. Then thought...Sasha?

There was a sudden pounding at the door.

"I hear them," she managed. "They're here."

"Are you able to let them in?"

She didn't answer. Just lay her head down and passed out.

51.

"Look at her throat."

Voices came to her, then hands, she felt hands tending her, cradling her head. "Get the neck brace on. Easy, defensive wounds can wait."

Feet moving, more voices as wheels rolled in, but her head reeled and her eyes refused to open. Much safer, here behind closed lids, safe and dark down here...no pain down here...

Sounds came clearer. The *snap* of an ironing board being collapsed to the floor...no, not an ironing board...one of those collapsible gurneys. Hello gurney, it's been a whole three months, gurney...

Strong hands lifted her, covered her with a light blanket, strapped her down. In the crowded murmur someone's hand was on her shoulder, and a voice said, "Three flights, another strap." She pictured them managing the gurney on the stairs.

Should have gotten an elevator place. The ridiculous thought came unbidden, probably mercifully. Minutiae were so much easier than the fact that your life as you knew it had just ended. Horribly. The final nightmare made real. So just allow in minutiae...or nothing. Later will be time to grieve, deal with – *no, stop it* – you're safe...and good people who save people have strapped you to an ironing board that's carried hundreds of others. Welcome back to the trauma club...

Liddy opened her eyes; saw the ceiling come closer as they raised up her gurney. She was dimly aware of Kerri arriving, trading brief exchanges with the others, then bending to her, hugging her gently. "Thank God. Your call was in the nick."

The lips were too dry to speak, but Liddy tried. "I never called," she whispered.

"Huh?" from Kerri, distracted by grim monosyllables filling her in about "the body;" and, "No *way* she could have struck from that angle;" and, "With that strength? She's a noodle."

Their voices floated out there, far from the dark comfort of eyes closed again: Kerri saying that other detectives were coming; they'd go over the room; someone else commenting about the force it must have taken to plunge in those scissors. Kerri's hand stayed on Liddy's shoulder. "I'm coming with you," she said, and Liddy opened her eyes to her, tried to smile; felt her face crumple and cried.

The gurney wheels were moving. Liddy saw the ceiling busy with shadows, activity, then the top of the door frame as they maneuvered through, then the living room ceiling, the dreadful white iron column. Kerri was by her side, comforting. Liddy tried to roll toward her. Kerri said, "Don't move, honey. You're pretty banged up."

The stairs, the stairs. Feet first and strapped in, strong guys on each side. Sometimes you just have to depend on others to carry you, but if they're good people... Liddy's eyes even closed stung and brimmed. "Hey," said a man's voice, reaching to wipe her cheek. "It's gonna be okay. You're okay."

"Thank you," she whispered.

The night was ablaze with emergency lights swirling. Liddy saw bright, winking stars and an almost full moon, and then – "One, two, three," she heard – she was hoisted into the ambulance to hands that got busy taking her vitals, swabbing her arm, starting her IV.

Kerri climbed in, sat on the bench next to her. Peripherally, Liddy saw a man in plain clothes appear too; stand over Kerri and reach for Liddy's hand.

"This is Alex Brand, my partner," Kerri said.

"Oh." Liddy smiled weakly. "You saved Kerri's life."

"We save each other," he said, squeezing her hand, sitting next to Kerri as the ambulance started to move. The siren sounded...such a safe sound. Liddy felt every swerve of the small Soho corners, and then they were really moving. Somebody mentioned Bellevue, which meant straight up First Avenue.

"Sasha..." Liddy breathed, straining at her gurney straps.

"Easy, hon." Kerri had one hand on her shoulder as her free hand pinged her cell phone. "I'm calling your friend Beth. She's your first in case of emergency contact?"

"Yes, thanks." *Not counting Paul. Never again counting Paul.* Impossible to believe, would she ever process it? Kerri's question and its answer were devastating; hearing her on the phone with Beth, loudly weeping and frantic, was a wrecking ball to the heart.

"She's okay, yes conscious," Kerri was saying. "May need a night in the ER for observation...Good, I'll tell her."

She disconnected. "Beth's on her way," she smiled encouragingly.

Alex told Liddy, "From the sound of it, you'll have to calm her."

She thanked them, but her heart felt ruptured, in real physical pain. So many dreams, that whole future, gone. But she had never known him, had she? Understanding who he was, what he'd done...that would take time. Years, maybe.

Sasha loomed up again, her silver, ghostly features going from rage to something softer, like peace. And then she vanished; Liddy heard the sound of singing from the studio.

Compulsion forced the words out. "He drowned Sasha," Liddy breathed, looking at both detectives. "Swam...out with her from the dock, let the current take her."

"He told you?" from Alex.

"When he was drunk that night. Lucked out that my concussion...I didn't remember."

She watched Kerri go limp with the sudden knowledge that it was over; her long, hard struggle was solved. They'd be needing more details...there'd probably be an attempt to retrieve what might be left of the body...but that, really was it.

"Whoa," Kerri said quietly, with her lips parted.

Alex held up a phone he'd been fiddling with.

"Yours," he told Liddy, looking confused. "You called Kerri, right?"

"No, I couldn't." The words came hard. "He knocked the phone away."

Kerri said, "I got your call at 7:38. Heard you screaming for help."

"I didn't make the call."

"Who then?"

The ambulance swerved. Liddy felt too drained for more; just managed, softly, "Sasha. It must have been her."

She closed her eyes, picturing the two detectives trading looks. She was in pain but her mind was sharp again; sharp enough to remember cops' voices saying *No way she could have struck from that angle*, and, *With that strength? She's a noodle.*

A noodle. That was funny.

They would take a while trying to figure it, and then they'd say, Well *something* explains it, the case is solved at least, that poor girl can be put to rest.

There was a final swerve, then feeling the ambulance climb a slight incline.

"We're there," someone said; and Liddy heard Kerri say, "That's it. Now I believe in ghosts."

"Put that in your report," Alex said teasingly.

"I plan to!"

They started going at it with each other, and Liddy smiled.

52.

They found her.

It took them four meticulous, grueling days in the murk and swirling current, but when they'd nearly given up one of NYPD's scuba divers searching nearly 70,000 square feet of the river bed was down in maybe a foot of visibility...and had the strangest feeling, he later told reporters. "It's like I *felt* it," he said. "I was pretty much on my stomach feeling around in front of my face, going back over the same rotted pilings I'd been over, and suddenly I just saw it - like what was left of it was waving to me in the current."

It was a piece of blue shirt, nine inches square roughly, tangled around river grass, some broken glass, part of a broken boat propeller, and part of a skull. Caught in the rotted edge of the shirt's fabric was a Winnie the Pooh ear stud.

Liddy had been there, watching, on the third and fourth days, and so had been present, behind the yellow tape, when they brought up the tangle. From where she stood, behind the docks, she had seen the exhausted, sad but relieved silence of the team as they bent over their find. A general murmur had gone up, detectives were called, and Kerri came to identify the ear stud.

"It's hers," she'd come to tell Liddy, tearful and hugging her, then returned to the divers on the dock.

The bone was a DNA match, it was confirmed thirty hours later, not that any cop felt they needed it.

And four days after that, on a Sunday, Liddy found herself standing at the edge of a stone wall, by the tumbling gate of a small cemetery in upstate New York. The others had left. Three cousins who'd barely known Sasha had found a small place near the grave of her mother, and there had buried her remains. There was no stone, though they'd told the few reporters present that there would be. Now there was just the freshly dug earth and a little pile of flowers, already wilting.

Liddy moved forward, and kneeled. Placed her plump, happy Winnie the Pooh bear holding his single white rose next to the wilted flowers. She reached, and arranged Winnie's duds: red boots and a little hooded raincoat over a heavy sweater, for colder weather. She'd gone to a children's clothing store for them.

"Rest, Sasha," she said. "Winnie's here to keep you company."

The little grave was silent, but somewhere near a bird sang, and Winnie smiled at her.

Sometimes, trying to sleep, Liddy thought back to the soft singing she'd heard that night from the studio. Her crazed fog of memory had finally realized: it was the theme song to "Winnie the Pooh." Now, softly, she sang it: "Winnie the Pooh, Winnie the Pooh, tubby little cubby all stuffed with fluff…"

Tears stung, so she stopped; peered up and around. The place looked so desolate. If once there had been grass it was now tall weeds studded by old, untended stones.

"Too cute," she heard behind her, and turned.

Kerri kneeled to the grave too; reached to pull Winnie's hood up over his head. "Heard it's gonna rain."

"Should I have brought a little umbrella?" Liddy asked.

"Nah, he'll be fine." Kerri leaned back on her haunches, sighing.

She'd become a friend. She, Alex and Beth had stayed till eleven that night in the ER, long after the two detectives had gotten their statement. Beth had come back the next morning with fresh clothes and orders for Liddy to stay at her place. She did. Kerri and Alex had been over twice after work - and they and Beth had talked, bringing solace about their own dark times, their coming to terms with starting life over.

Liddy hadn't been back yet to the loft.

"Nice and quiet here," Kerri said, watching tumbling clouds backlit by the dropping sun. Liddy stared at the wilted flowers, thinking of Beth two nights ago: "You gotta climb out, come out of this stronger, re-invent yourself. Isn't that what artists *do*?" She could be funny, stomping around waving her hands, and she'd been a friend long enough to be a real drill master when it came to pulling out of despair. That was the thing about good relationships: when one's down, the other's up and can help.

"You're going to be okay," Kerri said softly.

"Working on it."

"You'll come back. Different maybe, but okay."

Liddy nodded, and they were silent for a while. Kerri went back to watching the sky change to blooming rose with streaks of violet.

"We done here?" she finally asked.

"Yeah." Liddy raised her index finger to her lips, kissed its tip, and planted the kiss on Winnie's cheek. "Take care of Sasha," she said, and stood. Took a last look as Kerri rose too, then turned back with her to the gate.

Beth was waiting for them, and hugged them. Liddy put her arms around them too and melted into their embrace.

Beth started to bawl. "I *hate* cemeteries. Can we go now?"

Kerri between them took both their arms and they walked together, down the road a bit to the old Bronco. A cooling breeze blew in their faces; felt nice.

Driving, Kerri announced the time and said she'd have to break laws. Alex was making one of his great, ambitious dinners "and we don't want to be late," she said, taking a sharp, bucolic curve at fifty. "He leaves his creations in the oven to stay warm - only he forgets to turn down the heat so dinner burns."

Beth laughed. Liddy found herself chuckling too. Alex was going all out, he'd announced. Had picked wines and the "most sinful dessert" he could find; wouldn't tell what it was but still, what a warming picture: Alex sizzling good eats – the sound of life - in the pan. Liddy smiled, picturing it.

Kerri found *Sweet Home Alabama* on the radio, and turned it up a little. "Louder!" Beth yelled. Up further went the volume, and the joyous sound filled the car.

The Bronco roared around a left, headed into the sunset all streaks of peach and rose, and disappeared over the top of a hill.

Author's Note

Hello, and thank you for reading. If you enjoyed this book, I would love to ask you a favor to *please* spare a moment and leave a review for FEAR DREAMS on Amazon. It would mean so much.

If you do write a review, or a post on your favorite social website, I'd love to hear from you and thank you. Here's my Facebook page: https://www.facebook.com/JASchneiderAuthor

And Twitter: https://twitter.com/JoyceSchneider1

Or email me at Joyce@jaschneiderauthor.net

A new thriller's in the works, so please join my Newsletter at http://jaschneiderauthor.net You'll be the first to know when new books are available, and more!

Thanks again for reading,

Joyce

About the Author

J.A. (Joyce Anne) Schneider is a former staffer at Newsweek Magazine, a wife, mom, and reading addict. She loves thrillers... which may seem odd, since she was once a major in French Literature - wonderful but sometimes heavy stuff. Now, for years, she has become increasingly fascinated with medicine and forensic science. Decades of being married to a physician who loves explaining medical concepts and reliving his experiences means there'll be medical angles even in "regular" thrillers that she writes. She lives with her family in Connecticut.

61556219R00145

Made in the USA
Lexington, KY
14 March 2017